We were quite near the island now. ~~.....~~ great lump of a hill that rose in the middle, the whole place was dead flat. There didn't seem to be a single tree on it – not even a stump.

'Perhaps it's been used recently for bombing practice?' I couldn't help suggesting.

'Nonsense,' said Uncle Tristram. 'It is a wondrous sight. Wide and uncluttered. Perhaps the winters are quite harsh round here, so trees can't get established.'

'Blown away, are they?'

'Harry,' said Uncle Tristram testily, 'this island is famous for its rugged beauty.'

'So is the Gobi desert,' I snapped back, 'but no one goes there on hols . . .'

'A controlled riot of invention, with a plot that embraces everything (or so it seems) from pork pies (some on sticks) to man (boy)-made floods, Morning Glory's sweet flutings to ear-crunching accents, incontinent seagulls to all those hairy chins. A laugh on virtually every one of its 180-odd pages' CAROUSEL

ALSO BY ANNE FINE:

Published by Corgi Books:
THE BOOK OF THE BANSHEE
THE GRANNY PROJECT
ON THE SUMMERHOUSE STEPS
THE ROAD OF BONES
ROUND BEHIND THE ICE HOUSE
THE STONE MENAGERIE
UP ON CLOUD NINE

Published by Corgi Yearling Books:
BAD DREAMS
CHARM SCHOOL
FROZEN BILLY
THE MORE THE MERRIER

A SHAME TO MISS . . .
Three collections of poetry
PERFECT POEMS FOR
YOUNG READERS
IDEAL POEMS FOR MIDDLE READERS
IRRESISTIBLE POETRY FOR
YOUNG ADULTS

Other books by Anne Fine

For junior readers:
THE ANGEL OF NITSHILL ROAD
ANNELI THE ART-HATER
BILL'S NEW FROCK
THE CHICKEN GAVE IT TO ME

THE COUNTRY PANCAKE
CRUMMY MUMMY AND ME
DIARY OF A KILLER CAT
GENIE, GENIE, GENIE
HOW TO WRITE REALLY BADLY
IVAN THE TERRIBLE
THE KILLER CAT'S BIRTHDAY BASH
LOUDMOUTH LOUIS
A PACK OF LIARS
STORIES OF JAMIE AND ANGUS

For young people:
FLOUR BABIES
GOGGLE-EYES
MADAME DOUBTFIRE
STEP BY WICKED STEP
THE TULIP TOUCH
VERY DIFFERENT

For adult readers:
ALL BONES AND LIES
FLY IN THE OINTMENT
THE KILLJOY
OUR PRECIOUS LULU
RAKING THE ASHES
TAKING THE DEVIL'S ADVICE
TELLING LIDDY
IN COLD DOMAIN

www.annefine.co.uk

ANNE FINE

Eating Things on Sticks

Illustrated by Kate Aldous

CORGI YEARLING BOOKS

EATING THINGS ON STICKS
A CORGI YEARLING BOOK 978 0 440 86937 5

First published in Great Britain by Doubleday,
an imprint of Random House Children's Books
A Random House Group Company

Doubleday edition published 2009
Corgi Yearling edition published 2010

1 3 5 7 9 10 8 6 4 2

Corgi Books are published by Random House Children's Books,
61–63 Uxbridge Road, London W5 5SA

www.kidsatrandomhouse.co.uk
www.rbooks.co.uk

Addresses for companies within The Random House Group Limited can be found
at: www.randomhouse.co.uk/offices.htm

THE RANDOM HOUSE GROUP Limited Reg. No. 954009

A CIP catalogue record for this book is available from the British Library.

Printed in Great Britain by CPI Bookmarque, Croydon, CR0 4TD

For Geoff and Joe, the pioneers

The Plan

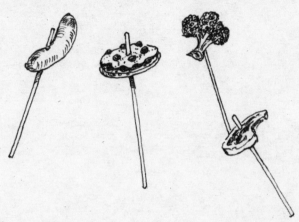

CHALLENGE ACCEPTED!

'No, no, no, no, no, *no*!' I said. 'Not to Aunt Susan's! Not for a whole week! No, no, no, no!'

Mum wasn't backing down. 'Frankly,' she said, 'I don't believe I have to listen to any complaints from the person who burned our entire house to a crisp.'

I had to defend myself. 'I did not burn the entire house to a crisp.'

I should have kept my mouth shut. Mum waved an arm around what little was left of our kitchen. 'Excuse me? Are these walls the cheery colour that they used to be, or are they *black*? I don't recall choosing this nice "charred wood" theme for the cupboards. Is that clean water gushing out of the tap, or some dark dribble of sludge from melted pipes? And aren't we lucky

1

that the sun's still up, because it's not as if, when I flick on this light switch, anything actually *happens*.'

'Look,' I said for the millionth time, 'I'm really *sorry*. I didn't *mean* to forget that I was making that toast. I didn't *realize* that I'd left that tea towel lying across the grill. And I did not *deliberately* forget we had a fire blanket.'

'What's to forget? The thing was hanging on the wall in front of you with FIRE BLANKET printed across its case in big red letters. You can *read*, can't you?'

'Yes,' I said sullenly. 'I can read. I just didn't *see* it, did I?'

'Apparently not. So now, when we try to make arrangements to find you somewhere to stay while the house is full of workmen, perhaps you'll stop whining.'

'I was not whining,' I said huffily. 'I was just saying that I didn't want to stay with Aunt Susan.'

Mum ticked our other conversations off on her fingers. 'Or with Aunt Miriam and Uncle Geoffrey. Or with Great-Granny. Or with next door. Or with–'

I interrupted her. 'Because it's not fair. Ralph gets to go to scout camp.'

'Ralph was booked in to go to scout camp already. More to the point, Ralph is a scout, and you are not.'

I threw myself on her mercy. 'Mum, please! Don't send me to Aunt Susan. I couldn't bear a whole week of her ghastly nature walks, and prissy little Titania prancing about in one of her frilly-willy frocks pretending she's a fairy and singing me one of her' – I did my imitation of my cousin Titania's lisp – '"thweet little thongs". Oh, please don't send me. Please!'

'Harry, there's no one else.'

I had an inspiration. 'What about Uncle Tristram?'

Mum stared. 'Tristram? You must be mad. Your Uncle Tristram couldn't look after a cat.'

Mum only said it as a figure of speech. Still, it reminded her of poor old Pusskins and what happened to him, so her face fell. I stood there sensitively for a moment or two before I said,

'But Uncle Tristram could look after me. Because I can look after myself.'

'But he won't want you,' Mum explained. 'It's his week off. He'll have arranged to go away with one of his girlfriends.'

'I could go with them.'

'I don't think Tristram would agree to that!'

'He would,' I told her confidently, 'if I asked.'

Mum laughed. 'Feel free to give it a try. Because otherwise you'll be off to Aunt Susan's first thing in the morning.'

Challenge accepted!

BLACKMAIL

'Sorry,' said Uncle Tristram cheerfully. 'No can do. Off on my own hols tomorrow.'

'Where?'

'Not sure,' said Uncle Tristram. 'Some tiny island, I believe. Only one ferry a day, or something. I admit that I wasn't really listening.'

'Why not?'

'Because,' said Uncle Tristram loftily, 'my mind was set on other things.'

I bet I knew what other things his mind was set on. 'So who is she, then?'

'Never you mind.'

I ran through Uncle Tristram's last few girlfriends. Jean with the grating laugh. Moira the bank teller who was forever counting her change. The acrobat called Flip. None of the stories ended happily. 'Well, do I know her?'

'No. She's new.'

'Does she have any . . .' Pausing, I finished darkly, '– *cats?*'

That shook him up. He started paying attention. 'Why do you ask?'

'Well,' I said, 'we wouldn't want any terrible accidents to happen, would we? And if any terrible accidents were to happen, just like to our poor little Pusskins, it might get harder and harder for me not to let drop to Mum – entirely by accident – that it was not the first time . . .'

'Harry,' said Uncle Tristram sternly, 'are you blackmailing me?'

'Yes,' I said. 'All I want is for you to offer me a roof over my head for one week. One tiny week! It isn't much to ask, and it will save me from being sent to Aunt Susan's.'

'To Susan's?' Uncle Tristram sounded shocked. 'Your mother's never really threatening to make you spend a whole week in the same house as that ghastly little cream puff Titania?'

'She is,' I said.

I could tell Uncle Tristram felt for me. He started cracking.

'If I did let you come, you'd have to look after yourself,' he warned.

'No problems there.'

'No hanging about, cramping my style.'

'I wouldn't dream of it. I'll bring my holiday homework.'

'And no more talk of Pusskins.'

'No.'

'All right, then,' said Uncle Tristram. 'Just to save you from Aunt Susan and a week with Titania.'

'Yes,' I said. 'Nothing at all to do with what happened to Pusskins.'

'Absolutely not.'

'That's right,' I agreed. 'In fact, I've practically forgotten all that sad business again already. Who was poor Pusskins anyway? And what did happen to him?'

He'd hung up.

Saturday

'GLERHUS DILL SOTBLUG'

Dad dropped me off at Uncle Tristram's flat. Before he left, he walked round Tristram's fancy yellow car, inspecting the state of the tyres. 'I suppose these treads are well within the legal limits?'

'Tickety boo, thanks.'

'I take it the brakes are adequate.'

'*I'm* still here,' Uncle Tristram said a little frostily.

'Yes,' Dad said. 'But this time you will be driving my son.'

'He isn't the *Messiah*,' muttered Uncle Tristram.

Dad has sharp ears. 'He might not be the Lord's Anointed, no. But he is precious to his

11

mother and myself. So you drive carefully.' He turned to me. 'Any doubts,' he warned. 'Any doubts at all, and you are to threaten to be sick on your uncle's upholstery, step out of the car the moment he screeches to a halt, and then phone home.'

'I'm not a *maniac*,' said Uncle Tristram.

'That,' said my dad, 'has always been a matter of opinion.'

And he drove off.

Uncle Tristram turned to me. 'I'm glad he's gone,' he said. 'I didn't really care for his attitude, considering I'm doing him and my sister a giant favour by letting you tag along with me and Morning Glory.'

'*Morning Glory?*'

'Now don't you start,' said Uncle Tristram, and he got in the car and waited while I climbed in on the other side and fastened my seat belt. Then he took off down the street, Granny-fashion, at about three miles an hour, until we'd passed the junction where Dad was lurking in his own car, hoping to catch us speeding so he could snatch me back and send me off for a week of nature walks with Aunt Susan instead. 'Fooled him, then,' Uncle Tristram said with satisfaction, speeding up. 'I hope he gets a ticket

12

for stopping on that yellow line.'

I stared out of the window. Huge supermarkets. Cinemas. Leisure centres. All shooting by. 'Where are we picking up Morning Glory?'

'We're not,' said Uncle Tristram. 'She is up there already.'

'Goody,' I said, because I like my times alone with Uncle Tristram. He's good fun. He doesn't stop at boring motorway cafes. He takes off 'till we find strange little restaurants in strange little villages selling strange little meals. He stops to moo at cows and oink at pigs. He suddenly decides we can't drive any longer without stopping for a go on the flumes in some big city pool.

It took all day and half the evening to get as far as the ferry. Ours was the last car to board. The man at the ticket office muttered, 'Glerhus dill sotblug,' before he gave us our tickets.

'What did he say?'

'How should I know?' said Uncle Tristram. 'I simply shoved a twenty-pound note under his little glass grille and hoped for the best.'

I think that hearing him say the word 'grille' must have reminded me of when I tried to make that toast. And that made me think of the fire. And that made me think of all the workmen who were trying to put the kitchen to rights. And that made me think of Mum and Dad, so I was a little bit homesick.

(Better than seasick, which came next.)

A WONDROUS SIGHT

'That is *disgusting*,' Uncle Tristram said, hastily moving upwind as I heaved the strange little meal from the strange little village restaurant over the rail of the boat. 'Here. Take this to clean yourself up.'

He reached in his pocket and pulled out his handkerchief. As I unwrapped it, out fell his mobile phone. It bounced on the rail. We both reached out to catch it and hit one another's hands instead. The phone splashed into the water.

Uncle Tristram swore wildly for a minute or two. Then he calmed down. 'Don't tell your mother you heard any of those words from me.'

'I promise.'

He gave me a bit of an evil look. 'Yes, well, we all know what *your* promises are worth. You said you'd never mention that stupid cat again.'

I felt too nauseous to argue Pusskins' case. (Excuse *me*, but Pusskins was only sleeping where he *usually* slept. A pet cat doesn't take his nap in a flower bed and actually *expect* someone to drive a Maverati through the petunias.)

And it had been a brand-new mobile phone.

So, 'I'm really, really sorry,' I said weakly. Then I threw up my pudding.

Uncle Tristram took pity on me. 'Perhaps you'd be better downstairs,' he said.

'Below decks,' I corrected. 'You don't say "downstairs" on a boat.'

Shrugging, he made for a big heavy door that led to some iron steps. Deep in the bowels of the boat, the other passengers were sitting hunched in gloom. Most of them had beards that you could hide your sandwiches inside – even the women.

'Why are they all in boots and mack-
intoshes?' Uncle Tristram whispered.

'Perhaps they know more about the weather
where we're going than we do,' I suggested
sourly. (I was still feeling rubbish.)

'Promph yarp ochellin?' one of the bearded
people suddenly suggested to Uncle Tristram.

'Quite so!' he answered with a somewhat
haunted look.

'Merpliddle fixam nop,' added another.

'Indeed, indeed.'

'Blerty ach nerp!'

Uncle Tristram stood up. 'Well,' he said cheerily, 'I think perhaps we'll have another small peep at the view from upstairs.'

'On deck,' I corrected.

'Whatever!' Uncle Tristram snapped, and led the way back up the iron steps. We were quite near the island now. Apart from one great lump of a hill that rose in the middle, the whole place was dead flat. There didn't seem to be a single tree on it – not even a stump.

'Perhaps it's been used for bombing practice recently,' I couldn't help suggesting.

'Nonsense,' said Uncle Tristram. 'It is a wondrous sight. Wide and uncluttered. Perhaps the winters are quite harsh round here, so trees can't get established.'

'Blown away, are they?'

'Harry,' said Uncle Tristram testily, 'this island is famous for its rugged beauty.'

'So is the Gobi desert,' I snapped back. 'But no one goes there on hols.'

He scowled. 'Would you like the return half of your ferry ticket now?' he said. 'Then you can take a train back down to Aunt Susan's.'

'No, thanks!' I said. I took another look. 'It's quite astonishing really. Look at the unspoiled sweep of it. Enchanting!'

'That's better,' Uncle Tristram said. 'Shall we start getting ready to get off?'

'Disembark,' I corrected.

But he'd already gone.

We were the only passengers to leave the boat at this particular island. 'Glerhus dill sotblug,' the ferryman warned once more as he let down the ramp so we could drive away.

'Quite so,' responded Uncle Tristram enthusiastically. 'Quite so. Quite so.'

MORNING GLORY

An hour later, we were still sitting in the car.

'It would be better not to have a map at all,' said Uncle Tristram, 'rather than one like this, that simply throws out the odd cruel hint as to where we might be.' He ripped it into pieces. 'I shall ask the very next person we come across.'

It was quite late by then, so there was no one. There were no houses, either. If there was a village anywhere, it was successfully hidden. We saw sheep, but they're not helpful when it comes to finding out where you are.

Finally, some ancient codger on a bike came round the corner. He had a beard like a used

scouring pad. I was expecting him and Uncle
Tristram to end up in yet another of the conversations like the ones on the ferry – all, 'Ooh, yar.
Darp plummet gep!' and 'Quite so. Indeed!' But
though the ancient codger was hard of hearing,
he clearly wasn't quite as steeped in darkest
dialect as those on the boat. So when Uncle
Tristram gave up on showing him the hastily
pushed together pieces of map and simply
shouted, 'Morning Glory!' at him, the baffled
look turned into a seraphic beam. Ushering us a
few yards round the corner, the ancient codger
pointed.

There, in the shadow of the hill we'd
seen from the ferry, stood what
looked like a large
and ugly card-
board box with
ill-fitting
windows.

'Marvellous!' said Uncle Tristram.

The codger stood there waiting for some sort of tip. But Uncle Tristram was already hurrying back towards the car. As he came past, he slowed so I could scramble in before he took off with a squeal of wheels.

IN THE PRESENCE OF THE APPLE

We knocked on the door. After a moment it opened, and there stood Morning Glory, dressed in some sort of silver tube that barely covered her bottom. Her legs were stuck in furry yeti boots. She wore a lot of bangles on one wrist, and flowers in her hair.

'Tristram!' she cried, and threw her arms around him.

'Hi, Morning Glory!'

he said enthusiastically, and patted her silver bottom. 'How far's the pub? Poor Harry and I are *starving*.'

'I'll fix you something,' she offered. 'Just let me finish my session first.'

'Session?'

'I'm putting myself in harmony with the universe,' explained Morning Glory.

Uncle Tristram asked guardedly, 'Does it take long?'

'No, no. You go and unpack.'

'I think we'll just sit here and wait,' said Uncle Tristram. (I think he hoped that we would put her off whatever she was doing enough to hurry things along.) Morning Glory sank cross-legged to the floor and sat there for a minute or two.

'What are you doing?' I asked her.

'Ssh!' she said. 'Try not to disturb me. I am sitting quietly in the presence of the apple.'

'What apple?'

She pointed. Over in the corner of the room, there was an apple on the floor.

'I'll bring it closer, shall I?' I offered politely.

'No, thanks,' she said. 'It's fine just where it is because, right now, I am just being *mindful* of the apple.'

'So you don't actually *want* it?'

'No,' she said. 'Not until it's time to look at it. I'll need it then. And after that, when I'll be *listening* to it.'

'Apples don't make a lot of noise,' said Uncle Tristram, 'unless someone's munching them, of course.'

'That isn't what I do,' said Morning Glory rather scornfully.

We sat and waited for what seemed a good few weeks while Morning Glory listened to the apple. Sometimes I looked around the room at all the lumpy brown furniture and a particularly ghastly corner in which there was a sizeable collection of owl and pig knick-knacks. The rest of the time I kept my eyes on Uncle Tristram, half expecting him to start making faces behind Morning Glory's back. But he sat tight. Clearly he'd had to sit through times when she did weird things like put herself in harmony with the universe before.

Finally, Morning Glory got to her feet and walked across to pick up the apple. She held it to her nose.

'What are you doing now?' I asked.

'Right now, I'm *smelling* the apple,' she explained. 'And after that I put it to my lips.'

'And will you eat it?'

'This is a Being-in-Harmony-with-the-Universe session,' Morning Glory said disdainfully. 'It's not a feast.'

She finished shortly after that, and unfolded upwards just the way our ironing board used to unfold before I burned it to a crisp. 'OK, I'm ready to go.'

Uncle Tristram jumped to his feet. 'Better make tracks. What time do they close?'

'Nine thirty,' Morning Glory said.

Uncle Tristram looked horrified. 'Nine thirty?'

'They're not a *real* pub,' Morning Glory said reprovingly. 'More a small family place where you can get light suppers.'

'But it's already ten! You should have *said*. If you had told us when we first arrived, we could have eaten by now.'

'The thing is,' Morning Glory said, 'that it's important, when you're in the presence of the apple, to let go of trivia like time.'

'What are we going to *eat*, though? I'm starving. And Harry here threw up his last meal. He'll be hungry, too.'

'I've got some nettle pudding,' Morning Glory said.

'What about the apple?' suggested Uncle Tristram.

Morning Glory looked shocked. 'We can't eat that! Not after I've been at peace in its presence!'

So we had nettle pudding. I can't say it was very nice, or that I'd ever want to eat it again. But it did settle my stomach. By then I was so tired that I went off to bed. Later, I woke to hear Uncle Tristram tiptoeing past my door and muttering to himself. It wasn't very clear to me what he was saying. But I did think that I distinctly heard the words 'could eat a weasel' and '*kill* for some chips'.

Sunday

NOTHING TILL SATURDAY

Next morning, when Uncle Tristram came downstairs yawning his head off, I asked him, 'Why were you wandering about in the night?'

'Impossible to sleep,' he said. 'I can't describe the length and misery of the hours. I had a terrible time.'

'The nettle pudding, was it?'

'No. The mice.'

'You never had mice for afters!'

He stared at me. 'Of course I didn't have mice for afters. They simply swarmed about my bedroom.'

'Mice don't swarm.'

'These did. They swarmed *all night*. I had to wrap myself in some old Chinese dressing gown of Morning Glory's, and huddle on the top of the chest of drawers.'

I looked around. The cold, bleak house. Uppity mice. Lumpy brown furniture. Pig and owl knick-knacks. 'Why did she choose this place to come on holiday?'

'We are the ones on holiday,' said Uncle Tristram. 'Morning Glory *lives* here.'

I was quite shocked. 'This is her *home*?'

'Yes.'

'But it is awful!' I burst out. 'There's nothing here. She hasn't got a telly or a DVD player. She hasn't even got a radio or a computer.'

'I suppose she likes the simple life.'

The door swung open. 'Hello!' said Morning Glory. She wore a sort of floaty kaftan thing and a frilly mob cap. Clasping her hands together, she made a sort of bow to each of us in turn. 'May the bright spirits of the day in me salute the bright spirits in you.'

'I don't think Uncle Tristram has bright spirits in him this morning,' I explained. 'He was attacked by mice.'

'Herded into a corner,' Uncle Tristram confirmed. 'Terrorized all night.'

'Silly!' chortled Morning Glory. 'If we are friends to them then mice are friends to us.'

I thought, since he'd been kind enough to bring me with him, I should stick up for my

28

uncle. 'My mother says that mice are vermin, and she puts out traps.'

Morning Glory gave me a pitying look. 'No wonder you were so desperate to escape up here with Tristram!'

I didn't dare say I was already desperate to escape back again. Instead, I asked her dolefully, 'Will we be having breakfast?'

'Before our walk?'

'Yes,' Uncle Tristram said firmly. '*Before* our walk. Let's go to the small family place. They will have bacon and eggs and stuff like that.' He turned to Morning Glory to wheedle some more. 'Then we won't have to use up any more of your delicious sorrel tea and precious dandelions on toast.'

She shook her head. 'You go. I have a few things to do here.'

'Righty-ho!' I could tell Uncle Tristram was relieved. I think he wanted to sneak out and buy some normal, everyday provisions before Morning Glory started frightening both of us by braising a squirrel or marinating road kill.

So off we went. As soon as we were in the car, he turned to me. 'Listen,' he said. 'I fear this trip was something of a mistake.'

'Mistake?'

'Well, yes. The problem is, I suppose, that you don't really know someone very well at all until you see them on their own home ground.'

Curious, I asked him, 'Did she seem normal at your house?'

'I suppose she did,' he said. 'But perhaps that was because there were no apples to be mindful of, and we were busy doing other things.' To cover his blushes, he let out the clutch and put his foot down. As we sped away, he told me, 'OK, here's my suggestion. We have breakfast, find out what time the ferry leaves, buy enough proper food to last us through the rest of the day, make our excuses to Morning Glory, and then we leave.'

'Top plan!'

We drove about. The little family restaurant had a sign on it: *Closed Until Further Notice*. There didn't seem to be a Waitrose. Or a Sainsbury's. No Morrisons. No Asda. Somertons was closed because it was Sunday morning.

In the end all we could find was the tiniest shop on the planet. It had four shelves and only one small fridge compartment which was barely as wide as the one that got melted at our house.

Uncle Tristram picked up one of the three battered wire baskets on the floor by the door and asked the bearded man behind the counter, 'When does the ferry leave?'

I think he must have been some sort of foreigner because we understood what he said.

'Saturday.'

The blood drained out of Uncle Tristram's face. '*Saturday?* Nothing till then?'

'They would have told you when you bought your ticket,' said the man defensively.

'Ah,' Uncle Tristram said reflectively. 'That would be "Glerhus dill sotblug."' He counted up the days to Saturday, and started filling the basket. There wasn't much of a selection, and most of that was pork pies. We bought most of them. I watched as Uncle Tristram stood gnawing his nails a little anxiously at the check-out. His card went through though, and we got away.

'Right!' he said. 'Pork pies for breakfast. Then I'm ready to face anything. Even a walk.'

A TELEVISION,
A DVD PLAYER,
A COMPUTER AND A RADIO

'First,' Morning Glory said, 'we have to tell our feet how much we appreciate them.'

'Why?'

She stared at me as if I were unhinged. 'Because your feet do lots of work for you. You have to thank your feet.'

'I've never thanked my feet before.'

Morning Glory ignored me. She sat on the floor and bent her body over to stroke her toes and heels while we pretended to copy her. 'Dear feet,' she said, while we did a bit of Amen-style mumbling along with her. 'We know how very committed you are to your daily task. We do appreciate that very much. We care about you. All today, we will be thinking of you.'

She wasn't wrong in that! All day I thought how sore my feet felt. She led us miles. Sometimes she stooped to gather scraggy green weeds and mucky-looking roots. Behind her back, Tristram kept winking at me as if to say, 'Well, you and I will not be eating *that!*' But I was not so sure because I'd come to think that Morning Glory was more than a match for both of us, and we were her guests, after all.

When we got home, we all sat on the sofa in a row. I thought I'd just check one more time. 'So you really don't have a telly?'

She shook her head. 'Not many people on the island bother. Since the last aerial blew down it's been such a pathetic signal that you can't even make out people's faces. Everyone looks exactly the same. They're all just grey and fuzzy blobs.'

'Well, what about getting a DVD player?' She looked a little blank. I thought I would step back in time a little. 'Well, don't you even have a radio?'

'No, Harry. I don't have a radio.'

'Or a computer?'

'No. No computer either.'

'Well, what do you *do* all day,' I wailed, 'except for picking weeds and thanking bits of yourself, and being in harmony with the universe?'

Morning Glory turned to me and smiled as if

I were some toddler who was getting overtired. 'Tristram,' she said to my uncle sweetly, 'would you mind fixing supper? Take Harry with you. I know he's missing his television and a few other things, and I've a plan to make him feel a little more at home here.'

'No problem,' Uncle Tristram said. I think, like me, he thought that she was off next door – wherever next door was – to try to borrow a few electronic basics. He set to with a will to make the sprout salsa while I got on with rinsing the weird lumpy roots and the watercress. On the sly, while Morning Glory was gone, we both ate four pork pies. I must admit I thought it was a little odd that neither of us heard the front door opening or closing after she left us or just before she returned. But that was all explained when Morning Glory finally came back into the kitchen and took my hand to lead me into the living room.

'There!' she said proudly, pointing to the wall.

I stared. On it, in thick black charcoal, she had drawn a television, a DVD player, a computer and a radio.

I didn't really know what to say, so I kept quiet.

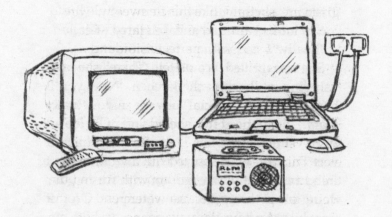

'Well?' she said, twinkling away as if she'd given me the keys to my very own palace.

I pulled myself together and tried to be polite. 'They're wonderful.'

'They are good, aren't they?'

'But they're not *real*.'

'Well, no,' she said. 'But does that matter? You're only here a week. It's such a lovely island it would be a waste of time to watch films, or play silly games on the computer. So these are simply to make you feel a little more at home.'

I wondered suddenly if it was possible to *swim* to the mainland.

'Well, thank you,' I said. 'No one has ever given me anything like this in my whole life.'

She looked amazed and delighted. 'Really?'

'Really,' I said with perfect confidence.

She was thrilled, I could tell. 'There!' she said, ushering me back to the kitchen. 'Now you'll have something special to write in your daily diary!' She noticed my baffled face. 'Oh, it's all right,' she assured me. 'I don't read minds. It was Tristram who assured me that you won't mind being left alone for hours if we're busy doing other things because you spend a lot of time keeping your daily diary.'

'He said that, did he?'

I turned to glower at Uncle Tristram, who was taking very good care to keep his head down over his chopped sprouts.

Monday

THE WALK TO LOOK
FOR ANGELS

Next morning for breakfast Uncle Tristram and
I had more pork pies. Morning Glory had barley
and mushrooms.

'Let's go and look for angels,' she suggested.

I gave Uncle Tristram a glance that said: 'She
is completely *insane*. You got us into this. You
get us out of it.'

He totally ignored it. 'Yes,' he said weakly to
Morning Glory. 'Let's go and look for angels.'

I glowered at him. I knew that he was only
saying it to try to wheedle his way into her good
books. 'Are you quite mad?' I hissed. 'You know
as well as I do that there are no such things as
angels. And even if there were, you would not
find them just because you go to look for them.

39

Even the people who believe in them know they live in a different—'

I couldn't think of the word.

'Universe?' Uncle Tristram suggested.

'*Realm*,' Morning Glory said. But I could tell that she had overheard and I had hurt her feelings. She went all quiet and started gathering up the pork pie wrappers and her bowl.

I tried to repair the damage. 'Well, I suppose there's no harm in just going to look . . .'

Her eyes went bright again. 'So you will come?'

'Not half!' I said enthusiastically. 'All my life I've longed to see an angel.'

'I have my own,' she told us.

Even Uncle Tristram looked startled at this claim. 'Really? Your very own angel?'

'Yes. She's called Dido and she hangs about at the top of the hill behind this house.'

'Hangs about?'

'In the air,' explained Morning Glory.

'Can anyone *else* see Dido?' Uncle Tristram asked cunningly.

'Only real true believers,' Morning Glory admitted.

'Oh, well,' said Uncle Tristram. 'Still worth the trip, I expect. Though it's a very steep hill.'

'Very,' I echoed.

It was, too. It took at least an hour to reach the top. Uncle Tristram and Morning Glory spent a lot of the time kissing and giggling on the narrow path. She'd come out wearing some sort of leopardskin tablecloth that trailed on the ground, but he had sent her back to change into the silver tube that barely covered her bottom. ('It'll get tangled in the undergrowth a whole lot less.') He made me walk in front, so I climbed very fast to spite them both.

I reached the peak. Only a little way down on the other side, water was bubbling out between stones. I reckoned it was far too high up the hill for any sheep to have got near enough to poo in it, so I knelt down to cup my hands and drink.

Finally, those two staggered up behind me.

'That is The Source,' said Morning Glory, pointing to where I was kneeling at the very start of the stream. We had studied rivers in school, so I looked down to see how it widened and deepened, and how one or two other streams joined it. Then I looked around for angels.

'Is Dido here yet?'

'Not yet,' said Morning Glory. 'Not till we call.'

She sat cross-legged and sang her Calling Angels Song. It went on quite a long time, so I wandered back to The Source and pushed stones around with my feet. When I came back up, Morning Glory had risen to her feet to start her Calling Angels Chant. That went on a bit as

well, so I drifted back to The Source and packed some mud around my new arrangement of stones. (If I was *four*, you would have called it spending my time building a dam in the stream. But I am well past four.) When I got bored with that, and came back up to the top for the third time, Morning Glory had stretched out her hands and embarked on her Calling Angels Entreaty. I can't remember much about the song, the chant or the entreaty, except that there was quite a bit about 'beloved feathered ones' and 'winged treasures of the world' and such stuff.

In the end, it was Uncle Tristram who glanced at his watch first. 'Should we be getting down again? I'm feeling quite peckish . . .' He trawled his brain for some more lofty reason to abandon the search for angels. 'And Harry here really ought to phone his mother to tell her what a nice time he's having.'

Morning Glory lifted her hand. 'Hark!'

I listened pretty hard, but I heard nothing.

Then, 'There she is! There!' Morning Glory was pointing into thin air. 'Oh, can you see her? Dido! You've come.'

Morning Glory dropped onto her knees. She held an animated conversation with the invisible (and silent) Dido, explaining who we were, and telling Dido how wonderfully radiant she looked. I stood to the side, like a spare pudding. Uncle Tristram took great interest in the stones beneath his feet, and we just waited.

At last, Morning Glory stepped forward with a wave. 'Farewell! Farewell, my angel!'

Eagerly she turned to Uncle Tristram. 'You saw her? You did see her?'

I watched poor Uncle Tristram paw the ground. 'I do think maybe I saw *something* . . .'

'She's *lovely*, isn't she?'

'Lovely,' said Uncle Tristram faintly.

I shouldn't have been grinning. I was next.

'You saw her too, didn't you, Harry? You saw her shining wings. You saw her glowing gown. You saw her radiant face!'

'Angels are beautiful,' I agreed.

I have to tell you I felt *brilliant*. I had been far more enthusiastic than Uncle Tristram, yet kept my dignity.

'Nothing can follow that,' I said to both of them. 'Shall we go down again now?'

THERE'S NO ESCAPE

When we got back to the house again, Morning Glory mysteriously disappeared.

'Stolen by angels,' suggested Uncle Tristram. But it was no more than a couple of minutes before he vanished as well. I spent a bit of time rooting through cupboards to see if I could find a pack of cards, or something else so ancient it didn't need a battery. But there was nothing.

So I did what Uncle Tristram had suggested earlier, and I phoned home.

My mother took the call. 'Harry! At last! We've phoned Tristram's mobile a thousand times but it's gone totally dead. Where on earth *are* you?'

I wasn't sure where Morning Glory was. For all I knew, she might be walking barefoot past the door. I didn't want to hurt her feelings again so I dropped my voice to a whisper.

'I'm on a tiny island,' I explained. 'There's no escape.'

'No escape?' Mum's voice turned anxious. She began to whisper, too. 'So where is Tristram?'

'I'm not sure.' In case he was with Morning

Glory, I added tactfully, 'But I don't think he's anywhere around.'

I realize now I must have sounded rather plaintive. Almost pitiful. Certainly I could tell from the change in her voice that Mum was getting more and more worried. 'Harry, who else is there?'

'Just someone Uncle Tristram thought he knew,' I explained, and couldn't help adding bitterly, 'But nowhere near well enough, it seems. And now it's too late.'

'My God, Harry! It's been three days! Are you even being fed?'

I'm not allowed to eat pork pies because of the additives. (Well, certainly not *four*.) So I slid round the topic. 'I did eat some nettles the day before yesterday,' I told her piteously. 'But only because I wouldn't have slept from hunger otherwise.'

Along the hall, I thought I heard a door open and a bit of giggling. 'Mum,' I said. 'Someone is coming. I don't have long to talk.'

'Quick!' she said. 'Tell me everything you can. Quick!'

'We drove for *hours*,' I said. 'Then we were rushed onto a boat. Everyone had accents. Really thick accents. We couldn't understand a word. And they have beards. There are no trees on the island and only one hill. I'm stuck inside now so I haven't really seen anything else.'

'Think!' Mum urged. 'Did you see anything – *anything* – on the journey?'

I thought back. 'Myrtledown Swimming Pool,' I said. 'And a strange little restaurant called The Woolly Duck.'

'Oh, good boy! Smart lad!' she said. 'We'll have you off that island in no time.'

'I really doubt it,' I said gloomily. Then I heard footsteps. 'I have to go!' I warned her. 'How's the kitchen coming along?'

'For heaven's sake, my precious! Don't you worry about the kitchen! It doesn't matter in the least! Don't even *think* about it ever again. Just hang in there and try to keep your spirits up.'

'All right,' I promised.

And when I put down the phone, I did console myself that even a day up a hill building dams like a toddler and looking for angels was better than being at Aunt Susan's.

Tuesday
and
Wednesday

BEARD TOUR

Next morning, Morning Glory brought me a cup of tea in bed. At least, I thought that it was tea until I sipped it.

'Splarrp!'

(I managed not to spit it on the counterpane.)

'Are you all right?' she asked me tenderly.

'Fine!' I said. 'Fine! What sort of tea is this?'

'One of my own blends. Catnip and marjoram.'

(Well, that explained it.)

'I have to work today,' she told me. 'I was just wondering if you and Tristram would like to come along.'

'I didn't know you had a job.'

'It's not a *real* job,' she explained. 'It doesn't

pay. But once a week I drive round dishing out the meals-on-wheels to the old people. I take the van down dozens of odd little cart tracks, and I thought it would be a very good way for you and Tristram to see a bit more of the island.'

I'd rather be grateful to a van engine than to my own tired feet, so I was up for it. 'When do we leave?'

'Straight after breakfast.'

That wasn't long. (She ate a parsnip pancake, and Uncle Tristram and I settled for pork pies again.) Then we piled into Uncle Tristram's car to get to the meals-on-wheels distribution centre.

Morning Glory pressed one of the buttons and her seat slid down. She pressed another. It slid up again. 'This is *luxurious*,' she said. She tugged her glittery woollen legwarmers up as far as her taffeta ballet skirt. 'Usually I have to hitch a ride to get to the centre.'

I didn't quite see how. The island was *deserted*. You'd think some plague had swept across the land and every living creature except seagulls had crept into a hole to die. Finally we reached the place where Morning Glory picked up the meals. It was a vast tin shed, almost a hangar, with wide-open double doors. Round

at the back, a van was parked outside. I thought
at first that someone had decorated it all over
with blobs of grey and greenish paint, but it was
bird mess.

Inside the shed there was a pile of packaged
trays, still cold from the fridge. Morning Glory
swept up the van keys one of the other
volunteers had left lying on top. 'We'll leave
your car here,' she told Uncle Tristram.

Uncle Tristram stared at the van, spattered
all over with droppings. Then he looked up.
The sky was swarming with seagulls and
helicopters. The seagulls were just waiting,
you could tell.

'I think I might just move the car safely
inside.'

We waited while he drove his yellow Maverati into the shed and then, as a special precaution against particularly nosy seagulls, closed the shed doors. Then we took off.

It was a tour of beards, really. The first lady only had a few proud wisps that floated on the breeze as she snatched her pile of meal trays and scuttled back into her cottage.

I started grumbling to Uncle Tristram. 'Yesterday, Morning Glory made us thank our feet for practically *nothing*. You'd think she might insist that rude old trout says thanks for a week's free grub.'

'Harry,' said Uncle Tristram, 'I fear that you and I are not the sort cut out for charity work.'

'Well, I'm not,' I admitted. 'I would be very tempted to snatch the trays back.'

Morning Glory drove on. The second lady looked more sinister. Her beard had matching eyebrows. She was unpleasant, too. When Morning Glory handed her the stack of trays she said, 'So what's it this week, eh? More of that foreign muck – all lumps of yak fat and camel lard?'

'I know that Thursday is macaroni cheese,' said Morning Glory helpfully.

'If I live that long,' muttered the foul old crone, hurrying back inside to bar-ricade the door in case any more kind people put themselves out to drive along her over-grown and rutted drive and offer her something for free.

'Blimey,' said Uncle Tristram once we were all three safely back in the van. 'That one could start a fight in an empty house.'

'Wait till you meet George,' Morning Glory warned.

We pressed on with the tour. Mr Appelini's beard turned out to be a spindly goatee. George had a 'bushy prophet'. He told me I was swim-ming in sin and would soon drown in sorrow. I asked him how he knew and he told me that you could see the face of the criminal in the

cradle. I said I wasn't *in* a
cradle. He said he could
still see that I was a bad
lot. I turned to Uncle
Tristram, expecting him
to stick up for me, only
to find that he was
narrowing his eyes
in my direction.

'Yes,' he agreed
with George. 'There is
a sort of born malefac-
tor look about his phys-
iognomy. And he's already a skilled arsonist.
Burned down his mother's kitchen only last
week.'

'I wish you'd stop harping on about that,' I
snapped. 'It was an *accident*.'

'The typical criminal defence!' scoffed
George.

I left them both agreeing and stormed back
to the van. Then we drove on to Mrs Mackay's.
If you were fair, she didn't really have much of
a beard at all, and was only a bit 'back to
nature'. Mr Fisher's beard was all over the
place, and curly with it. Old Joe's was brilliant
– sort of forceful and wild, all at the same time.

56

Ted Hanley's beard was thicker than a hedge and looked as if it might have fledglings nesting inside it. He actually said, 'Thank you.' I didn't hear the words myself, but Morning Glory and Uncle Tristram both swore to it. It made their day.

'The Devil has a beard,' said Uncle Tristram as we got back to the main road. 'A spiky little number, as I recall.'

'I like the wild ones,' I admitted. 'I can't *wait* to be old enough to grow one as all over the place as Old Joe's.'

'Don't grow a beard,' said Uncle Tristram. 'They're shifty and unhygienic.'

'And tickly,' said Morning Glory.

'How do you know?' asked Uncle Tristram. 'Have you been kissing any of your meals-on-wheels clients?'

Morning Glory shuddered. 'No.' She turned all wistful. 'But I did have a boyfriend once. He had a beard until he had to shave it off for his new job.'

'There you go!' Uncle Tristram trumpeted. 'Shave for Success!' He patted Morning Glory's legwarmers. 'Are you sure you're not getting too warm in these?'

'There's only one more house,' said Morning Glory.

It was a hovel really. Standing in front of it watering his tomatoes was the hairiest man we'd seen that morning. Straggling grey locks sprouted in all directions. The beard went down to his knees.

'Impressive,' Uncle Tristram observed. 'Brutish, yet somehow thoughtful. Barbaric, and yet shapely. Yes, I think that this one takes the prize.'

Morning Glory turned round to stare at Uncle Tristram as if he'd just solved some massive problem that had been troubling everyone on the island for years.

'Prize for the best beard?'

Uncle Tristram shrugged. 'If you could herd the pack of them together. To me, they looked a rather antisocial lot. Especially that one who told Harry he was swimming in sin and would soon drown in sorrow.'

'They'll all be at the fair, though.'

Uncle Tristram stared. 'What fair?'

'The Annual Island Fair on Saturday.' In her excitement Morning Glory bounced up and down. 'We always need a special competition. Best Beard is perfect.'

'Why can't you do the usual things?' asked Uncle Tristram. 'You know. Firmest fruit. Tastiest vegetable.'

'Not this year.' Morning Glory shook her head. 'We've had West Island Pulp Rot.'

'Finest carved turnip?'

'The school had a knife amnesty only last month and took away all the sharp ones.'

'Best dress-up?'

'We used to do that, but I always won without even entering, so they got rid of it.'

'So are there any competitions left?'

'Only the Eating Things on Sticks competition.'

'Eating Things on Sticks?'

'Yes,' Morning Glory said. 'You know. The

usual. Sausage on a stick. Cream puff on a stick. Pizza on a stick. Toffee apple on a stick. Fish finger on a stick—'

Uncle Tristram had already stuffed his fingers in his ears, but I kept listening.

'Hot dog on a stick. Steak on a stick. Ice lolly on a stick. Pork pie on a stick—'

'Did she say pork pie on a stick?' asked Uncle Tristram, taking his fingers out of his ears and looking interested again.

Morning Glory kept chanting. 'Salami on a stick. Chocolate fudge on a stick. Meatballs on a stick. Frozen banana on a stick. And, of course, pickle on a stick.'

I couldn't help asking, 'Do you get toppings on your frozen banana?'

'You get a choice,' said Morning Glory. 'They're chocolate-dipped, of course. But on top of that you can have sprinkles or chopped nuts.'

'Brilliant!' I turned to Uncle Tristram. 'Can we go?'

He looked a little pale. 'It's cutting it fine with the ferry.'

'Not really,' Morning Glory said. 'The fair begins at ten. The ferry doesn't leave till six. You can eat everything by then.'

'But Harry here gets seasick.'

'I wouldn't!' I insisted. 'Not if the things I'd eaten were *on a stick.*'

Uncle Tristram shrugged. 'I suppose it's like the growing-a-beard thing. Everyone has to make their own mistakes before they come to their senses.'

We gave the hairy man his week of meals, and drove back to the storage centre to drop off the van. There were still helicopters buzzing overhead.

'Better than seagulls,' Uncle Tristram said. And while Morning Glory phoned the organizers of the fair to suggest a Best Beard competition, he trailed around the shed until he found some old tarpaulin to drape over the bright yellow roof and bonnet of his car in order to protect them on the drive home.

A FLASH OF ANGEL'S WINGS?

Early next morning, Uncle Tristram picked up his camera and strode to the door. 'We're already halfway through the week and I don't have a single photograph.'

'Take one of me!' said Morning Glory. She

pranced around the kitchen in her bare feet and nightie.

'No,' Uncle Tristram said firmly. 'Your charms last all day long. It's only nature that looks better in early-morning or evening light.'

He turned to me. 'Coming?'

'Not bothered,' I muttered.

Uncle Tristram took one more look at Morning Glory flouncing about in her nightie. 'Well, I *am*, I'm afraid,' he said. 'So you come with me.'

Sighing, I heaved myself off the hard little wooden chair and followed him out of the door. I stood about while he fussed with his lens cap and zoom and light filters and whatnot.

'Why are you doing this anyway?' I asked him. 'It's not like you to go outside to take photos of hills and countryside when you can stay in and take photos of girls in their nighties.'

He tapped the side of his head. 'A cunning plan,' he said, 'to show that I, too, am in harmony with the universe.'

'Oh, I see. So we won't be out for long?'

'Barely a moment.'

He aimed the camera up the hill. I waited for the click.

'Odd,' he said suddenly, lowering the camera. 'It looks a bit different.'

'Different?'

I looked up the hillside. It looked just the same to me. Steep. Barren. Just a shade too close.

'I can't see anything.'

'Look,' he said. 'Right up there at the top. Can you see something glinting?'

I said sarcastically, 'Oh! Could it be a tiny flash of angel's wings?' and added my imitation of Titania: 'Thooper, Uncle Twithtram! Can we go and *thee*?'

He was too busy looking up the hill to pay attention. 'You know, I do believe it's water.'

'Can't be,' I told him. 'The stream runs down the other side.'

He handed me the camera. 'You look,' he ordered. 'Use the zoom.'

I twiddled until everything came into focus. Sure enough, there was a tiny stream of water trickling down the hill.

'Strange,' Uncle Tristram said. 'You'd think you'd need a heap of rain to cause a second stream like that to come down on our side. Unless there is some kind of blockage at the top, of course.'

I felt a slight twinge of unease.

'Maybe we should just climb up there again today,' I said. 'To check things out.'

'Check things out?'

I didn't feel like mentioning the dam I'd made. I thought he might tell Morning Glory, and she would tick me off for inharmoniously meddling about with the universe. So I said, 'You know. Just to look for angels.'

He gave me a stern look. 'I know she's *loopy*,' he said. 'But she is very sweet and very kind.'

'And very pretty.'

'And very pretty. And I am getting very fond of her. So let's have no more teasing about her angels.'

'Fair enough,' I said.

ONE QUICK BURST

I meant to sneak off up the hill by myself, but Morning Glory turned out to have plans. 'Today I thought we could drive over the island together to see my father,' she told us.

Uncle Tristram had left off trying to prove he was in harmony with the universe and taken to

64

setting all the pig and piglet knick-knacks in battle order against the owls. 'I think I'll just give that a miss,' he said. 'But do feel free to take young Harry with you.'

'If you don't come with us, we'll have to hitch,' warned Morning Glory.

'Borrow my car.'

'Brilliant!' said Morning Glory. 'I've never driven a car as sleek and powerful as yours. Up until now, I've only ever puttered about in meals-on-wheels vans and the odd rusty police car.'

I wondered if I'd heard her right. 'Did you say *police* car?'

She turned a little shifty. 'Only fetching chips.'

I still thought it sounded odd, unless she was an undercover officer. But Uncle Tristram wasn't even listening. He was still busy setting out his owl and pig attack lines.

I didn't really fancy dying in a quite unnecessary car crash. I shoved my face in front of his to make him pay attention. 'If Morning Glory isn't used to powerful cars, Mum would be furious if you let her take me out with her on her very first time.'

He rolled his eyes. 'Oh, all *right!*' Moving a

winsome little china owlet into her battle position on the dado rail, he made one last weak stab at sending us off without him. 'What is your mother's line on hitchhiking?'

'She is one hundred per cent against it,' I explained to him. 'If she found out, she'd kill me. Then she would kill you.'

'That rather robs the safety aspect of forbidding it of some of its punch,' said Uncle Tristram. 'But I do take your point. Either we all three go, or Morning Glory hitches alone.'

'What?' I said. 'Wearing *that*?'

Uncle Tristram turned from his knick-knacks. 'Isn't she even *dressed* yet?'

'Yes,' Morning Glory said. 'This is a *day* dress.'

'Sorry,' I said. 'But it is very thin and airy, isn't it? I thought it was another of your nighties.'

Uncle Tristram sighed. 'Whatever she calls it, it's still an invitation to being pestered by strange men in beards. I suppose that means we'll all three have to go.'

'Goody!' said Morning Glory. 'I'll go and drag those filthy old pieces of tarpaulin off your nice car.'

Uncle Tristram looked anxious. 'There will be

seagulls. Shouldn't we leave them on?'

Morning Glory's face fell. 'It seems a shame,' she said, 'to have a beautiful yellow car and drive around looking more like a moving haystack.'

'Better than having to spend the week chiselling off seagull poo,' said Uncle Tristram. He went to rope the pieces of tarpaulin even more firmly over his Maverati while Morning Glory and I packed up some dandelion fritters and a few pork pies.

Then we were off. The helicopters were all over again.

'Somebody lost at sea, I expect,' said Uncle Tristram.

'Then why are they buzzing about all over the island?'

'Are they?' He poked his head out of the open window and craned upwards. 'So they are. Maybe they're after bank robbers.'

'There are no banks on the island,' Morning Glory said.

'Car thieves, then?' Uncle Tristram suggested.

'They won't want this one,' I assured him. 'With these tarpaulins draped all over it, it looks like a corporation tip on wheels.'

'Still,' Morning Glory said wistfully, 'it would be nice to have a *little* go at driving it . . .'

Now he'd been dragged away from all his owls and pigs, it seemed that Uncle Tristram was far less keen to hand over the wheel to someone who had so far only trundled down a few cart tracks in a meals-on-wheels van, and used a rusty old squad car to fetch chips.

'As you so rightly said,' he started pontificating, 'this is a very powerful car. I'm not at all sure that it would be safe.'

'Please?' Morning Glory pleaded. 'One really quick *burst*?'

He winced. 'No, no. I know that Harry's mother wouldn't like it.'

How two-faced can you get? He had been keen enough to let her loose when it was only my life on the line.

68

To spite him, I said, 'I could always get out,' and added mischievously, 'After all, fair is fair! Morning Glory did take us all the way up the hill to look for angels.'

'Oh, all right,' he rather surprised me by agreeing. 'You get out of the car. That'll be safer. Indeed, I think your mother would insist on it. We'll drive back down the road the way we've come, just for a while, then turn round and meet you' – taking revenge, he pointed to a sheep pen about a hundred miles away – 'over there.'

I know when I've been trumped. Unbuckling my seat belt, I got out of the car and set off walking. The two of them changed places, and with a clash of gears and only one or two short roars of horror from Uncle Tristram, the car spun round and took off fast the other way. From time to time, I glanced back over my shoulder, but they were nowhere to be seen.

I reached the sheep pen at last and sat in its shadow, sulking. Finally – *finally* – after I'd had enough time to grow one of the Uncle Joe beards that I'd been fancying so much practically down to my feet, I saw them driving back.

LUCKY ESCAPE

'We had a lucky escape there,' said Uncle Tristram.

I was so cross I just pretended I couldn't care a fig about anything or anyone Morning Glory had nearly run into or over. But he pressed on. 'This police officer suddenly leaped out from behind a hedge and flagged us down.'

Now this did interest me. 'Did he have a beard?'

Uncle Tristram stared. 'No,' he said finally. 'Now that you come to mention it, he was clean-shaven.' There was a long, long pause while he glanced suspiciously at Morning Glory as if, like me, he was remembering what she had said about one of her old boyfriends having to shave off his beard. Then he pressed on with his story. 'Anyhow, he peered at me for a very long time – sort of *inspected* me.'

I was still feeling sour. 'Probably wanted to know what sort of person is so obsessed with bird poo he drives round with tarpaulins draped all over his Maverati.'

Uncle Tristram adopted a lofty look. 'I don't think he noticed that. He simply nodded curtly at Morning Glory, peered into the car, and asked me to step out and open the boot for him.' He snorted. 'I actually had to *explain* to him that you don't have to step out of a G46 Turbo Maverati Ace-Matic in order to get the boot open.'

I gave up sulking and climbed back in. 'So what was he looking for?'

'I don't know,' Uncle Tristram said. 'I thought at first he was just pouncing on us because Morning Glory had been driving so fast.'

'I was not,' Morning Glory insisted. 'I was just *tootling*.'

'Tootling in *this* car,' Uncle Tristram pointed out, 'can often amount to what an officer of the law will call "excessive speed".' He turned to me. 'So then, of course, I was all "Oh, Officer this," and "Oh, Officer that".'

'Turned into a bit of a crawler, you mean?'

'Put it your own way,' Uncle Tristram snapped. 'In any case, as soon as Morning Glory saw the two of us standing together, she was out of the car in a flash.'

'And then?'

'And then, of course, this meddling police officer found himself doing nothing more than staring at her nightie.'

'It is a *day* dress,' Morning Glory insisted.

'You call it what you like,' said Uncle Tristram. 'All I can say is that it *worked*. He clean forgot about her irresponsible and reckless driving. He went beet-red, took a quick peek in the boot to see if we were hiding some missing child it seems that everyone's looking for, then waved us on.'

I wondered if it was the moment to ask Morning Glory if this was the very same officer who used to lend her his rusty squad car to fetch chips. But she was standing with a bright pink face, scuffing a few bits of dried seagull poo into a heap on the road with her luminous satin slippers.

I turned back to Uncle Tristram and asked instead, 'So are we going to her father's or not?'

'Yes, yes,' said Uncle Tristram. Just to show off how safe a driver he could be himself, he took an age to do a simple three-point turn – making great play of craning his head in all directions and checking his mirrors ten times in a row.

Then we were on the road again.

BIT GLOOMY

'So what's he like, your dad?' I asked Morning Glory when we had gone a few miles down the road and she'd recovered from her embarrassment.

'Bit gloomy,' said Morning Glory. 'You mustn't let him get you down.'

'Has he a beard?'

She looked at me as if I had asked something like, 'Does he have *feet?*' So, yes. Another beard. I settled comfortably in the back seat and let my mind drift. Mum had as good as *ordered* me not to think about the kitchen, but still I wondered what colour she had chosen for the new cabinets and whether we would get another microwave or keep the old one, even though you have to press the buttons dozens of times before it obeys you.

When I woke up, the car was bouncing down a stony track towards some sand dunes. On the right was a cottage so ancient it was half sunk in the ground. Outside stood some fearsome codger of at least a hundred. He had the best beard yet – it looked like a forkful of straw after a three-day tempest.

The codger shook his fist at us as we rolled past.

Morning Glory waved back. 'Hi, Dad!' She turned to Uncle Tristram. 'You have to stop here. This is it.'

'Here?' Uncle Tristram asked, horrified. (I think that what he meant was *'Him?'* but it wasn't polite to come out with that.)

Morning Glory scrambled out of the car and ran across to throw her arms round her father. 'Daddy! It's been such ages. I've missed you so much.'

A snort shot out of the beard. 'Self-pity never boiled a haddock.'

I looked at Uncle Tristram as if to ask, 'What's

that to do with anything?' and he shrugged back. Then, 'Look at the man,' he whispered. 'His face is miserable enough to make a funeral procession turn up a side street. You'll have to rescue the poor girl. Hurry up. Get out of the car and be cheerful.'

'Why *me*? Where are you going?'

He hummed and ha-ed, and in the end the only thing he could come up with was, 'I'm going to find somewhere to park, away from the seagulls.'

'We're at the *sea*,' I pointed out. 'Over there are the *sand* dunes. That is the beach. There will be seagulls everywhere.'

'Just get out,' Uncle Tristram said, 'and earn your keep. Say happy things till I get back.'

I scrambled out and went to stand beside poor Morning Glory. 'Oh, what a lovely beach!' I said. I clasped my hands together in delight, just like Titania does when someone asks her to recite one of her ghastly poems or sing one of her ghastly songs. 'Look at the way the sun is glittering on those waves!'

Her father said despondently, 'Aye. But don't forget that midsummer is less than a spit away from the start of next winter.'

I took a deep breath. 'But it's nice today!'

'For each summer morning, we've a bitter winter night to come.'

'Cheer up, Dad,' Morning Glory urged. 'At least I've made it over here.'

He gave a listless shrug. 'One visit more, one visit less.'

'Oh, come on,' Morning Glory wailed. 'You mustn't start to think about how many times we'll ever get to see each other again. You'll live for ages yet!'

'Maybe I didn't mean myself,' said Morning Glory's father, adding morosely, 'Don't you forget, my precious, the bonniest flower is often the first to wilt.'

I gasped. But Uncle Tristram had given me a job and I thought I should at least be making a stab at doing it when he came back. So I said cheerfully, 'Morning Glory *is* pretty, isn't she?'

'Fair hair can hide dark roots,' he warned. 'Her sins will have to go down in the book of No Rubbing Out, along with everyone else's.'

Morning Glory looked horrified, burst into tears, and I gave up.

FARTING DONKEYS

It was Uncle Tristram who rescued us. Striding up manfully, he seized Morning Glory by the arm and led her away. Hastily I scuttled after them. 'What's up?' I heard him asking her. 'Don't tell me your dad's upsetting you already?'

Still weeping, she nodded.

'He's told her that she's going to die soon and she'll go to Hell,' I sneaked to Uncle Tristram.

Uncle Tristram stared. 'I was away two minutes!' He strode back to Morning Glory's father and put on a beaming smile. 'Well, absolutely lovely to have met you, Mr . . . ?'

'McFee,' growled Mr McFee.

'Of course! McFee. But really we only popped in to invite you to join us at the island fair on Saturday.'

'Look for me that day in my bed,' said Mr McFee. 'I'll probably have my face turned to the wall.'

'Don't want to see the farting donkeys?' Uncle Tristram asked.

'I don't.'

'Or have your head licked by the Arabian camel?'

'No, I do not.'

'You could enter the Eating Things on Sticks competition.'

'No, thank you.'

'Oh, well,' said Uncle Tristram cheerfully. 'Sadly, we have plans for the rest of today. But should you change your mind on Saturday, you'll find us at the fair, eating our things on sticks.'

He ushered us down the track to where he'd parked the car inside some bushes.

'*Will* there be farting donkeys?' I asked eagerly.

'I doubt it,' Uncle Tristram said.

'What about a head-licking camel?'

'Oh, do grow up!' said Uncle Tristram. 'Can't you see I was just trying to ease the three of us out of the old man's doleful gravitational field without being rude?'

'Oh,' I said, disappointed. 'But there will be eating things on sticks?'

'Yes,' Morning Glory assured me. 'There will be eating things on sticks.'

We all piled back into the car.

'Well,' Uncle Tristram said. 'That visit went well, didn't it?'

I leaned forward to ask Morning Glory, 'If

your dad's as gloomy as all that, how come he even agreed to let you have the name you do?'

'What do you mean?'

'Well, "Morning Glory"! It's such a cheerful, optimistic name.'

She cocked her head to one side. 'I suppose it is,' she said, as if she'd never given it a thought before. 'But, there again, everyone says he used to be a very cheerful, optimistic man.'

'Really?'

'Yes,' Morning Glory insisted. 'I'm told by everyone that he was "a veritable sunbeam".'

'*Him?*'

'Yes.'

'So what went wrong?'

'It's a sad story,' Morning Glory said. 'He was a really good runner. Championship standard, Mum says, and everyone agrees he had a chance at running in the Olympics. But he was so busy training, he ran right past the notice board down at the ferry terminal every day for a month and never slowed up long enough to read the signs plastered all over it. And Mum had just had me, so she had not been out much and hadn't heard about the changes in the timetable. So it was only when he went down to the terminal to get to the mainland to compete in his heats that he found out that his ferry had been cancelled.'

'Well, there you go.' Uncle Tristram shook his head with the wisdom of bitter experience. 'Glerhus dill sotblug.'

'That's right!' said Morning Glory. 'And ever since that day when my father missed his one and only chance of winning something wonderful, he has been miserable. That's why my mother ran away to the other side of the island. She says she'll never think of coming back until he smiles again.'

'That is a *tragic* tale,' said Uncle Tristram. We sat in respectful silence for a few seconds, and then he added, 'I really think we ought to cheer ourselves up a bit. What shall we do?'

'Is there a cinema on the island?' I asked.

Both of them looked at me as if I'd asked, 'Is there a Disneyland?' We settled for a walk along the beach. Uncle Tristram and Morning Glory strolled on ahead. He put his arm round her, and kept on leaning closer to dry her tears about her gloomy father, or kiss her or something. I was so far behind I couldn't really see. At one point I felt cross enough to shout at them, 'This is so boring it could be one of Aunt Susan's ghastly *nature* walks.'

The wind was gale force, though. My words were blown away.

TELL ME! GO ON! TELL ME! TELL ME!

On the ride home, I asked them curiously, 'How did you two meet?'

Both of them looked embarrassed.

'Go on,' I pushed. 'Tell me.'

'It's just too silly,' Uncle Tristram said. 'I'd feel an idiot telling you the story.'

'So would I,' Morning Glory said.

I thought she'd crack first, so I started on her. 'Go on. Go on. Tell me. Go on. Please! Tell me! Tell me!'

'For God's sake,' Uncle Tristram said. 'Just tell the boy before I push him out of the car.'

So Morning Glory told me the story of how she'd begged a ride to London after an argument with someone on the island.

'Your dad?'

'No.'

'Who, then?'

'Not telling,' she answered petulantly.

'Just give me one small clue. Did he have a beard?'

She plain ignored me. I didn't push my luck.

'OK,' I said. 'You went to London in a bit of a snit.'

'I was not in a snit,' she said. 'I was bereft!'

'That's how I found her,' Uncle Tristram said. 'The poor girl was sitting on her suitcase, weeping. I offered her a place to stay.'

'Only so long as I got rid of that spider.'

'What spider?' I asked Morning Glory.

She grinned. 'The one that was keeping him out of his bathroom.'

'The thing was *massive!*' Uncle Tristram said. He spread his arms to show me. 'It had been squatting there for days!'

'It was a money spider,' Morning Glory said. 'Tiny. I stayed a week.'

'Was it a week?' said Uncle Tristram. 'It seemed to pass in a *flash.*' He leaned back to say to me airily over his shoulder, 'Then that morose bearded maggot we just made the mistake of visiting sent her a note.'

'What did it say?'

'I can't remember,' Uncle Tristram said. 'Perhaps a few tribal curses. Something about the stern path of duty. The road to London is the shortcut to Hell. That kind of thing.'

'He told me to come back for Aunty Audrey's funeral,' Morning Glory said. 'While I had gone, she'd died of a heart attack and left me the house.'

'This one we're staying in?'

'That's right.'

Scales tumbled from my eyes. 'So all that lumpy brown furniture and stuff is your Aunt Audrey's, not yours? All of those knitted pigs and china owls?'

'Some of the pigs are crocheted,' said Morning Glory. 'And one or two of the owls are made from a rather fine terracotta.'

'I'm going to make them have their Grand Battle soon,' said Uncle Tristram. 'My money's on the pigs.'

'The house *is* very gloomy,' Morning Glory admitted. 'But it is *famous*.'

'Famous? Why is it famous?' I couldn't help asking.

'Because it has the only tree on the island.' She turned, astonished. 'Haven't you even noticed it? That apple tree in the garden? People come miles to see it.'

'Really?' said Uncle Tristram.

'Wouldn't you?'

83

'Not really, no,' he admitted. 'Trees are a bit "two a penny" where I live, I'm afraid. I don't think I'd go any distance at all to look at a plain old apple tree.'

Morning Glory shrugged. 'Well, I must confess that, much as I love the apple tree, up until recently even I was thinking of selling Aunty Audrey's house and moving somewhere else.'

'Where were you planning to go?'

She turned all wistful. 'There is a lovely cottage overlooking the fairground. Not very far away from the police station.' Morning Glory sighed. I thought I heard her muttering, 'Though that dream's over now.' But just at that moment we came round the last bend and there the house stood in front of us. Squat and dark and bleak.

Ghastly, in fact.

We all sat staring at it, swathed in the pall of gloom that seemed to have followed us all the way back across the island. In the end, Uncle Tristram broke the silence by asking, 'But who would ever *buy* it? It may have the only tree, but who would want to buy a house on any island with no bank, a ferry only once a week, and not a single cinema?'

I had an idea. 'Someone who likes eating lots of things on sticks?'

Thursday
and
Friday

PING! PING! PING!

When I woke up, the rain was beating on the windowpanes. The sky was grey. I could hear dripping and see little pools of water all over my uncarpeted bedroom floor.

I hurried downstairs. Morning Glory was on her knees, rooting in the back of a cupboard.

'Have we got any buckets?' I asked her. 'My room is springing leaks.'

'We're clean out of buckets,' she told me. 'Already this morning we've used up most of the saucepans. We're down to mixing bowls now, and Tristram says if any more leaks start up we'll be reduced to tea cups.'

I ate a pork pie on a stick. (I had begun to practise.) And then I helped by wandering round the house like Tristram, emptying saucepans and buckets.

Ping! Ping! Ping!

'The upstairs of this house is like a colander,' he kept on grumbling. 'We're going to have to stay home all day simply to keep an eye on it.'

I peered along the landing. *Ping! Ping! Ping!* The floor was cluttered with mugs and jugs and cereal bowls, all filling fast.

'I've got an idea.'

I went back downstairs to the cupboard in which I hadn't found anything modern enough to use a battery. What did folk do all day before things with batteries were invented? Chopped logs and knitted? And sure enough, on the top shelf I found a basket overflowing with balls of leftover wool of every colour and shade.

On the shelf below there was a packet of drawing pins.

'All we need now is a ladder.'

We found a pair of folding steps out in the coal shed. Then Uncle Tristram held them steady for me while I climbed up and down with lengths of coloured wool and drawing pins. It took an hour or so, but finally I'd managed to use the pins to stick one end of each of the lengths of wool into the ceiling plaster right beside every spot where drips kept bulging. The drips ran down the wool instead of dropping off. We gathered all the bottom ends and draped them all over the rim of one big bucket.

'There you go!' I said. 'Down to one bucket in the middle of every room. And no more pinging!'

Morning Glory clasped her hands together. 'My heavens, that is so beautiful! It looks like an upside-down maypole.'

'Brilliant!' said Uncle Tristram. 'I think your new system buys us just enough time to get our breakfast.'

We had more pork pies on sticks. It was too wet to go out. I got so bored I started on my holiday homework: *Imagine you are Frankenstein's monster, suddenly endowed with feelings. Write your daily diary.*

'What does endowed mean?' I asked Uncle Tristram.

'Given,' said Uncle Tristram. 'Like Morning Glory got this house from her Aunt Audrey.'

I knew I'd end up having to copy the whole thing out a second time in best, so I didn't bother writing out the title. I just got stuck in.

> Sunday: The strangest day. I feel as if I have been given a new life. Everything seems brighter here. I stare down at the clumps of grass outside the door. They shine like scattered emeralds among the rocks. I gaze at the sky. It glows like the bluest sapphire. Is it me, or have I moved into a different world?

Easy-peasy, once you let yourself go.

> Monday: This morning I woke fearing the magic might have vanished and I'd be back to my same old dull grey plodding self. But, no! Again today I seemed to walk on air. The mice scurried as I strode with heart aloft between the dark walls of this place. I think they sensed my growing confidence.

I snuck out for one more pork pie, and licked the stick as I carried on.

Tuesday: I've seen an angel! Speak to me last week and I would have told you she was nothing more than a pretty young lady. But I see more clearly now. She is a shining angel! I want to shout to those around me, "Look at her! Don't you see her radiance?" But I know better than to spill my secret. So I said nothing.

Uncle Tristram came into the room. 'What are you doing?'

'Nothing,' I said, tucking my work away safely behind the sofa cushion.

'Well, stop your slacking,' he told me, 'and come upstairs to take your turn emptying buckets.'

I'M GOING TO NEED SOME MONEY

We got ahead with the emptying, then took a bit of time off to get lunch and practise with things on sticks. First we had comfrey fritters. (Don't even ask.) Then we had florets of broccoli. (They were hard to stab.) Then we had artichoke pancakes. (They were all floppy and you almost had to slide in underneath to get them eaten.)

I could see Uncle Tristram working himself up to ask Morning Glory a question. Finally, out it popped. 'Have you *always* eaten like this?'

'What, off a stick?' Distracted, she let her pancake slither down inside her velvet bodice. 'Don't you think, if I had, I'd be a little better at it?'

'I didn't mean that,' Uncle Tristram said. 'What I meant was, have you always eaten this sort of stuff?'

'What sort of stuff?'

He spread his hands. 'You know. All these weird gleanings from' – he tried to suppress a shudder – 'the *countryside*. These comfrey fritters, for example. And those turnip croquettes that we had yesterday.'

'The parsley muffins,' I added bitterly. 'And that nettle pudding.'

Morning Glory turned huffy. 'Oh, I know! Down in London you eat good stuff like pizzas and hamburgers and sushi and samosas and sweet-and-sour chicken and—'

'Stop!' I interrupted her. (I was practically *drooling*.)

'Well, you have *restaurants*,' said Morning Glory. 'And money. You can *afford* to eat like that.'

'Not *much* money,' Uncle Tristram argued.

'You have a whole lot more than me,' said Morning Glory.

I felt a little guilty. After all, we had been with her since Saturday night. She hadn't had a single one of our pork pies, and we'd had lots of her stuff.

'I am owed pocket money,' I pitched in. '*If* I'm still getting it after burning down the kitchen. I could phone Mum and ask, and if I am, maybe we could lash out on steak and chips and I could pay you back later.'

She didn't argue, so I went in the living room and phoned home.

Mum picked up instantly. I could tell she was in a state. 'Harry! Thank God! Are you all *right*, my precious?'

'I'm fine,' I told her.

She didn't believe me, you could tell. 'Really?'

'Well,' I admitted, 'I can't say it's much fun. I'm really cold, and I am sick of emptying buckets.'

I heard her whispering, 'Poor lamb! They've got him in some sort of cell! He's even emptying *buckets*.'

I looked round Aunty Audrey's living room. 'It isn't quite a *cell*,' I said. 'But it is damp and bleak.'

'Oh, my poor darling!'

I thought it might be time to strike. 'I've had to ring you, I'm afraid, because I need some money.' Realizing instantly how bad it sounded, only bothering to get in touch in order to beg for my allowance, I made a little joke of it. 'That's if you want me out of here alive!'

Mum made a choking noise and said, 'You just put one of them on the line!' I wasn't going to drag in Uncle Tristram or Morning Glory to do my wheedling for me. 'I can't do that,' I told her, horrified.

'Well, how much are we talking about?'

I thought about it. 'The whole lot, I think.'

'The whole lot? What does that mean?'

I couldn't *believe* she had forgotten yet again how much I get each week. 'It's—'

I heard a creaking noise behind. Distracted, I turned to see the precious only apple tree on the island outside the window gradually keel over sideways and crash to the ground, taking the phone wire with it.

GONE DOWN SOME POTHOLE

Poor Morning Glory was *distraught*. 'The tree! The tree!'

We all went out to look. Uncle Tristram thought to snatch up Morning Glory's umbrella with the dancing frogs to save her velvet bodice and cowboy skirt from getting wet. But he and I just stood there getting drenched.

'How did it *happen*?' she wailed, mystified.

'It is strange, I admit,' said Uncle Tristram. 'Because it isn't even windy.'

'The ground feels odd,' I said.

It did, too. Where I was standing, there was a sort of sodden wet roiling and boiling, as if the earth beneath my feet was churning into mush. 'The hill looks different,' Morning Glory said. We all looked up. I felt a stab of guilt. I had forgotten to sneak up to unblock my dam, and now the stream was tumbling down our side of the hill as firmly and as strongly as if that were its natural route.

For all his earlier wavings of the camera at the glories of the view, Uncle Tristram didn't

95

seem to have noticed that the stream had switched sides.

'If there were ever any sun to glint in,' he observed, 'that water might look quite pretty till it suddenly disappears like that, halfway down.' He shrugged. 'Gone down some pothole, I expect.'

We stood there, shivering, till Uncle Tristram finally dared interrupt Morning Glory's Farewell Lament to her fallen tree by saying, 'Can we go back inside? I'm soaking. And we really ought to get back to the buckets.'

OWLS v. PIGS

At tea time it was still raining hard, so Uncle Tristram arranged a rota. I emptied for an hour, then Uncle Tristram took a turn. As it began to get dark, Morning Glory took over.

'I know,' said Uncle Tristram as soon as the two of us were alone. 'Let's have the battle of the pigs and owls. Cheer ourselves up. Bags I command the pigs.'

'I wanted to be owls in any case,' I told him.

We had a great time. Pigs were flying every-

96

where. The owls were vicious. I had them crawling across the curtain rails and up and down chair legs. Now that we knew it wasn't Morning Glory's furniture, we felt a little freer to clamber over sofa arms and climb on the sideboard to fetch a piglet down from where he'd been spying from some light fitting, or shove a pack of owls into formation on top of the nest of stools.

I had my advance force abseiling down the dresser when one of my knitted owls unravelled a little on its descent and fell in a drawer.

'Man down!' crowed Uncle Tristram.

'Not so!' I countered, and mounted a rescue. One of my china owlets went down inside the drawer to fetch out her companion in arms.

The knitted owl had got all tangled with some envelope. I brought them up together.

Just at that moment, Morning Glory came back at the end of her shift. 'Your turn again,' she said to me.

'Can't stop,' I warned her. 'Owls on the counterattack.'

'You *have* to stop,' she said, 'because I am not carrying on emptying buckets just because you two are mucking about.'

'We are not "mucking about",' said Uncle

Tristram. 'We are engaged in a ferocious and deadly duel of skill and cunning. If I am not at my most committed and focused as a commander, his evil owlets may take over the world.'

'It's still his turn to do the buckets,' Morning Glory said.

I know when to give up. I rose to my feet in front of the dresser. 'Want this?'

I handed her the envelope.

'Is it for me?' She snatched it so keenly I knew she must be desperately hoping for some particular letter. But then she saw it was already open, and her face fell. She pulled out the papers inside. 'Oh, it's just Aunty Audrey's house insurance.'

'Is it still valid?' asked Uncle Tristram.

She took a closer look. 'Only until the end of the month.' She sighed. 'So that's another bill that's winging its way towards me. And I must say, now that the tree's fallen over, I just don't feel I have the same commitment to the place.'

'If you'd prefer to have the insurance money,' joked Uncle Tristram, 'just ask young Harry here to set the place on fire. He's good at that.'

I blushed.

Morning Glory looked around. The damp

was seeping halfway up the walls now. There was a sort of tidemark around the room.

'I doubt if anyone could set fire to somewhere as damp as this.'

'It doesn't matter anyhow,' I told her loftily, 'because I'm afraid that I only do kitchens.'

HEY! DRESS-UPS!

At nine o'clock the rain stopped. To celebrate, I had a wild mint samosa on a stick. An hour later, the dripping upstairs had slowed its pace enough for us to go to bed. I had a troubled night, dreaming of helicopters circling overhead, the powerful beams of their searchlights sweeping across the panes of my bedroom window.

When I came down in the morning, there was a giant heap of clothes piled on the sofa.

I picked up an old-fashioned corset with so many laces it could have made a whale look trim. 'So what's all this lot?'

Morning Glory sighed. 'I've just been round to check on all the buckets, and there was water seeping out of one of the cupboards.'

'*Upstairs?*'

'Yes. I think the apple tree must have pulled down some of the guttering as well as the phone wire when it fell over.'

I looked around. The tidemark of rising damp was far, far higher up the wall. I nearly said, 'All the wet in this house is soon going to meet in the middle,' but Morning Glory looked so defeated, standing there in her tutu and tartan wellingtons, clutching her beaded pashmina round her shoulders. So I tried to distract her by picking up the next thing on the pile – a long black sequinned gown for someone as big as a house – and saying, 'You must have lost a huge amount of weight since you wore this.'

'Don't be so silly,' Morning Glory said. 'These clothes belonged to Aunty Audrey.'

I held up a little girl's frock. It was the sort of daft cream puff affair Titania would prance around in. 'What, even this?'

'Aunty Audrey kept *everything*, right from her early childhood. Some of the clothes in this pile must be eighty years old.'

'They'd fetch a fortune in London.'

She stared at me. 'What do you mean?'

I held up another frock. Nothing but frills and furbelows and scallops. 'Plenty of shops in London sell antique stuff like this. My mother's always strolling past and scoffing at the prices.'

'Really?'

'Really.' I dived in the pile. 'Look! You've got matching shoes and handbags!'

'Would they sell too?'

'Of course they would,' I assured her. I waved an arm towards the knick-knack corner. After the grand battle, it had been reduced to a few semi-unravelled owls and a couple of badly chipped piglets. But it still proved my point. 'There's always someone who will pay for any old rubbish.'

'I suppose you're right.' She sighed. 'It would be lovely to have a bit of extra cash . . .' No doubt remembering that my attempt to get some had ended when the phone line was dragged down, she shrugged. 'Oh, well. Better start thinking about breakfast.'

'Are there no more pork pies?'

'Not quite enough,' she said. 'I'm going to eke them out with a few dandelion rissoles.'

'That'll be nice,' I said faintly as she went off to the kitchen.

'What'll be nice?' asked Uncle Tristram, coming in a moment later.

'Dandelion rissoles for breakfast.'

He made a face. 'Are there no more pork pies?' Glancing into the living room, he saw the clothes on the sofa. 'Hey! Dress-ups! Excellent! When it starts raining, we can play charades.'

When, he said, you will notice. Not just *if*. When.

'You have to be careful,' I warned, following him back into the room. 'Morning Glory is planning to sell them in London.'

'Not till we've had some fun.' He rooted through the pile. 'Where's all the men's stuff?'

'There isn't any,' I explained. 'It all belonged to Aunty Audrey.'

'Oh, well.' He tore off his pyjama top and dropped a huge lace frock over his head.

'We have the matching shoes for that,' I told him as he struggled into it.

'Really?' As soon as he was covered by enough billows of black lace, he modestly turned his back and stepped out of his pyjama bottoms.

'What about tights?' I suggested.

'What *about* tights?' he asked me, dangerously.

'I'm only dressing up, you know. I am not strange.'

'Shoes, then?' I handed him a pair like boats. He stepped into them with no trouble. 'She must have had enormous feet.' He tottered around the room. 'Hand me my bag, please.'

I found him something fetching in sequins and jet.

'What about you?' he said. 'You're no fun standing there in boring old trousers and sweater.'

'Oh, all right.' And, if I am honest, I was bored enough to be quite keen. So I dug through until I found the cream puff frock again. I even went one better than Uncle Tristram, and pulled on some knee-length little-girl white socks and shining Mary Jane shoes.

'Your hair's all wrong,' he warned me.

'So is yours.'

So we went back to digging in the pile until I found a lace mantilla for me to drape over my head, and a perky hat for Uncle Tristram that had so many feathers sticking out of it that you couldn't tell he had short hair underneath.

'Now don't we both look splendid!' Uncle Tristram said. 'Let's go and give Morning Glory a laugh.'

VERY UNWELCOME VISITOR

We wanted to surprise her, so we crept down the hall. It took a bit of time because of Uncle Tristram's heels. I thought I could hear banging, but just assumed that it was something to do with crushing dandelions. Only when we got closer did we realize that someone was knocking angrily on the back door.

'Morn! Morn! You let me in!'

I was about to prance forward anyway, but Uncle Tristram stopped me. He raised a finger to his lips, then pushed the door a little further open so we could spy on what was happening. Morning Glory was frying rissoles, totally ignoring the racket behind her.

'Morn! I'm on official business here, so you let me in at once!'

'You go and boil your head, Tom Watkins!' Morning Glory said.

'Don't be so rude! And you should be calling me Officer Watkins, not Tom! I haven't come about anything personal. I represent the law.'

'You represent your own silly self,' scoffed Morning Glory. 'That door's not even locked. And mind you wipe your feet before you come in here, or you'll be mopping up after yourself on your way out.'

I whispered to Uncle Tristram, 'Shouldn't we go in?' and added, though it seemed unlikely, 'She may need a little *help*.'

Uncle Tristram glanced down at his black frock and shoes and handbag, and then across at me, dressed in my cream puff. 'Maybe creep back and change first?' But he was clearly far too curious to leave his spying place, so we just stood there through what sounded like a very thorough scraping of Tom Watkins' feet.

Finally, in he came. No beard!

Uncle Tristram gave me the nod that meant, *Yes! This is the very same officer who flagged me and Morning Glory down on the trip across the island.*

Officer Watkins took off his cap. 'You've let that garden I dug over become a mud bath,' he complained to Morning Glory.

'I didn't *let* it,' she snapped. 'I could hardly *stop* it, since it rained all last week and all the week before and it was raining all day yesterday.'

'It hasn't *stopped*, you know,' said Officer

Watkins sarcastically. 'If you look out of the window, you might notice that it's still raining now.'

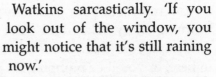

'Good,' Morning Glory said, 'if that means *you* get even wetter.'

We turned to raise our eyebrows at one another.

'So!' Uncle Tristram breathed. 'Do we suppose this is the old boyfriend who dumped her?'

'It certainly sounds like it,' I whispered back. 'Perhaps we shouldn't eavesdrop.'

'No,' Uncle Tristram said. 'We should just tiptoe away at once.'

He made no move.

Inside the kitchen, the very unwelcome visitor reached in the frying pan for a dandelion rissole. Morning Glory slapped at his hand.

'Oh, go on,' Officer Watkins said. 'You know I love your grub.'

'Crawler!' I heard Uncle Tristram muttering beside me. 'Why is that man here? What on earth does he want?'

'Rissoles?' I whispered.

'Oh, do be quiet!' Uncle Tristram hissed. 'I'm trying to *listen*.'

'I'll tell you why I'm here,' said Officer Watkins (rather conveniently) to Morning Glory. 'I've come to search your house.'

'Search it?'

'Yes,' Officer Watkins said importantly. 'For missing persons.'

'Well, you should recognize *them* easily enough,' said Morning Glory. 'Being a bit of one yourself.'

He glowered at her. 'What's that supposed to mean?'

'Where were you on that Saturday night?'

'At the *dance*,' Officer Watkins snapped. 'I hung about for hours, waiting for you.'

'Oh.'

I pushed the door a little further open, so we could both watch Morning Glory turn beet-red.

'And speaking of missing persons on that same Saturday night,' said Officer Watkins, 'where, I might ask, were *you*?'

'I was at home,' said Morning Glory, 'waiting to be picked up.'

'I *couldn't* pick you up,' said Officer Watkins. 'I couldn't get the squad car because Delia needed it to fetch the chips. I told your dad to *tell* you.'

'That was a little daft of him,' hissed Uncle Tristram, 'to trust that miserable sad sack with any message that might lead to some fun.'

He must have hissed it just a little too loudly, because Officer Watkins suddenly turned. 'Who is behind that door?' he asked suspiciously.

'No one,' said Morning Glory. (I think she must have panicked.)

'Really?' asked Officer Watkins. 'Because the other day you did appear to be out and about with' – he spat the words out quite aggressively – 'a brand-new *boyfriend*.'

'No, I was not,' said Morning Glory. 'That was some smoothie-chops estate agent who happened to pop over to value the house before I try to sell it.'

I looked at Uncle Tristram. Uncle Tristram looked at me.

Officer Watkins persisted, rather unpleasantly, 'So what were you doing in his car? Dressed in that nightie?'

'It was a *day* dress. And he was simply giving me a lift to my dad's.'

'Letting you *drive*?'

'I wasn't driving. I simply mentioned I was planning to buy a car like his. He was just letting me sit in the driving seat to see how it felt.'

'At forty miles an hour!'

'I pressed the wrong thing. Then my foot slipped on the pedal.'

'I might believe you,' Officer Watkins offered, 'if, when I search this house, I find he isn't here.'

'He's not!' said Morning Glory, sounding desperate.

'Well, let me look then. Then I'll believe you, and we can make up and go to the fair together.'

'We can make up and go to the fair together anyway.'

I looked at Uncle Tristram again. He looked at me.

'That sort of settles it,' I whispered. 'You are quite definitely second-best.'

'It does seem that way,' he admitted ruefully. Then he cheered up. 'Mind you, there's always this Delia . . .'

Inside the kitchen, Officer Watkins was pressing home his advantage. 'Anyhow, it doesn't matter what you want. We have two missing persons on this island. One of them is probably already dead, and the other is definitely kidnapped. We're searching *everywhere*. And this house is next.'

He tried to push his way past Morning Glory, who thought to distract him with a kiss. It must have been very long kiss, because it gave us more than enough time to creep back down the hall, and while we were on our way I thought about all of Uncle Tristram's other hopeless relationships, and all the speeches I had ever heard my mother make to him.

Then I made this one for her. 'Listen,' I whispered sternly. 'She's much more in love with him than you are with her. And he loves her back. He even likes her grub. And you and Morning Glory have nothing in common. Nothing. Just think about it. She might even want you to live on this island! So I certainly hope

that for once you're going to be sensible, and do
The Right Thing.'

THE RIGHT THING

As Officer Watkins burst into the living room a
few moments later, Uncle Tristram put out his
hand and trilled, 'Good morning! Allow me to
introduce myself. I am Aunt
Susan.'

Morning Glory stared.

Adjusting his feather
hat, Uncle Tristram
pressed on in what he
clearly took to be an
aunt-like fashion.

'And from the look
of you, you are a Man
of the Law! Could you,'
he simpered, 'by any
chance, be the delight-
ful PC Tom Watkins of
whom we have heard
so much from our dear
Morn?'

111

Now Officer Watkins was looking as startled as Morning Glory.

Uncle Tristram turned to me. 'Here,' he said, 'is my precious little daughter Titania. Say hello to Officer Watkins, dear.'

I reached up to make sure that my mantilla was in place. 'Hello,' I chirruped. And then, since Uncle Tristram had lumbered me with ghastly Titania's name, I thought I might as well take on her personality as well. 'Thall I thing everyone a little thong?'

'Beg pardon?' said Officer Watkins.

Uncle Tristram moved slightly so he was standing between me and Morning Glory's boyfriend. He slapped my head, hard.

'That would be lovely, dear,' he trilled. 'You sing like an angel. But now is not the time. Officer Watkins is busy.'

I grasped a fistful of cream-puff frock on either side and did a curtsey. 'How about a vewy quick danth, then?'

'No,' Uncle Tristram said.

I cocked my head to one side and took a stance. 'One little rethitation? I know a thooper little poem about a thongbird who gets trapped in a greenhouse and gradually thtarves to death.'

112

Uncle Tristram leaned over to kiss me. 'You precious little duck!' he carolled. Then he hissed in my ear, 'You will be dead yourself if you don't watch it.'

I thought I'd better watch it.

Uncle Tristram turned back. 'Well!' he warbled. 'I'm sure Officer Watkins has work to do. Houses to search, and such . . .'

That seemed to bring our visitor to his senses. He started looking under chairs and peering around suspiciously. 'Bit of a mess in here,' he mentioned, pointing to the heaps of clothes on the sofa.

'Oh, don't mind that lot,' Uncle Tristram chirruped. 'Dear little Titania and I are still unpacking.'

'What about all these bits of wool and broken ornaments? Has this room seen some kind of *fight*?'

'No,' I said. 'I wath jutht playing a little game

with thome of the knick-knacks. You thee, I thent the little china pigs off to the fair, and then thome very naughty owls flew over and they—'

Once again, Uncle Tristram stepped between me and Officer Watkins and surreptitiously cuffed me.

'Anyhow, a lot of them got thmashed and torn,' I finished hastily.

Officer Watkins peered in the cupboards in a businesslike manner. Then he went to the door.

'I'll search upstairs now.'

'While you are up there,' Uncle Tristram cooed, 'would you be a perfect treasure and empty the buckets?'

Morning Glory followed Officer Watkins out of the door and up the stairs to the landing. Even before the two of them were out of earshot, they had taken up their quarrel.

'I *said* I heard voices,' Officer Watkins grumbled. 'Why did you tell me there was no one there?'

'Why should I tell you anything?' said Morning Glory. 'You're not still my boyfriend.'

'Yes, I am.'

'*Are* you?'

'I am if you *want* me to be. Do you?'

'Only if *you* want to be.'

'Of course I want to be. You *know* I love you. You know I always have.'

'And I love you as well.'

Uncle Tristram got up from his armchair and pushed the door shut so he didn't have to hear them kissing. He turned to me. 'I hope you're satisfied. Now I have to sit here in this stupid frock until those two have finished billing and cooing.'

I jumped to my feet just like Titania would at any such opportunity. 'I could thing you a little thong! Or do a little danth!'

He grinned. 'You're very good at imitating her.'

'I've had a lot of practice – not with the frock!' I added hastily. 'Only the voice.'

'Well, go on,' Uncle Tristram said. 'Amuse me. Do that stupid poem of hers about those pathetic kittens who run away from home and die in a snowstorm.'

'*It wath a dark and fearthome night?*'

'That's the one.'

'All right.' I climbed on the coffee table and, bunching the sides of my frock in my hands, curtsied before simpering, 'I'm going to rethite for you a very thad thtory.'

Already Uncle Tristram was shaking with laughter.

I clasped my hands together and began the poem that we'd been forced to sit and listen to politely only about EIGHT BILLION TIMES.

'It wath a dark and fearthome night.
The kittenth lay thafe in their bathket.
To go outthide would cauthe them fright.
No one would even athk it.'

'Appalling!' Uncle Tristram crowed with glee. 'Simply appalling. Oh, don't stop, Harry!'

I carried on. It's a long poem. I was still in the middle when Officer Watkins and Morning Glory came back in. He had his arm around her waist, and they were giggling.

Uncle Tristram raised a finger. 'Hush, hush!' he warbled. 'While we were waiting, my dearest Titania here embarked on a short recitation. May we just hear her out?'

Officer Watkins sat down politely. Morning Glory sat on his knee and tickled him behind the ears as I pressed on.

'Then, through the thnow and through the thleet
The little kittenth picked their way.
All dethperate to find a plathe
Where they could thyelter till the day.'

116

Around the tenth verse, Uncle Tristram suddenly covered his face with his hands and rushed out. And as I reached the very last two lines –

'Came to their mother as a fearthome blow
To thee thothe little corptheth in the
thnow.'

– I could distinctly hear behind me, through the hole in the windowpane caused by some kamikaze piglet, the sound of roars of laughter that could not possibly have been made by anybody's *real* Aunt Susan.

MY DAILY DIARY

Finally – *finally* – Officer Watkins tore himself away from Morning Glory and made for the door.

'Now don't forget tomorrow at the fair!' he told her gaily, stepping out into the garden. Instantly both his shoes sank so deep in the mud he nearly lost them. Prising them upwards, one by one, over and over with a series of horrible sucking noises, he gradually picked his way towards the gate.

'I ought to dig a drainage ditch through this back garden,' were his last words. 'No wonder your apple tree fell over. This place is turning into a swamp.'

Uncle Tristram and I went back into the living room and scrambled out of our frocks. 'I saved your bacon there,' said Uncle Tristram sternly to Morning Glory.

She looked repentant. 'Do you mind? Horribly?'

'I mind,' said Uncle Tristram. 'But not *horribly*. Much as I have adored you, I could no more live on this benighted island than fly to the moon.'

'What's *wrong* with the island?' demanded Morning Glory.

'Don't even start!' I hissed at Uncle Tristram. 'Remember she no longer loves you, it's pouring with rain, and there is still a heap of time before the ferry gets us out of here.'

He took my point. Pretending he was too busy clearing Aunt Audrey's clothes off the sofa to get into an argument, he let the matter drop. After a moment, Morning Glory pitched in to help. We heaved the piles of shoes and dresses and corsets tidily into a few massive rubbish bags, and sat down to play cards. Morning Glory kept wriggling. 'I'm so uncomfortable!' She reached behind her and tugged out the whalebone corset and the holiday homework I'd stuffed behind the cushion and clean forgotten.

'What's this?'

She glanced down at it. Then she looked at me. Tears sprang into her eyes. She gave a little sob. Then, turning to Uncle Tristram, she told him haughtily, 'At least there's *someone* in your family who appreciates the beauty of this island, and is in harmony with the universe.'

In blatant astonishment, Uncle Tristram pointed in my direction and said, 'Who? *Him?*'

She cleared her throat and read aloud the first words of my holiday homework.

'*Sunday: The strangest day. I feel as if I have been given a new life. Everything seems brighter here. I stare down at the clumps of grass outside the door. They shine like scattered emeralds among the rocks. I gaze at the sky. It glows like the bluest sapphire. Is it me, or have I moved into a different world?*'

She raised her eyes and looked at me with love and admiration. 'This is your daily diary, isn't it? And this is how you felt on the first day you came! I'm moved and touched.'

Behind me, I heard Uncle Tristram mutter, 'Certainly *touched*.' I was quite worried they'd get in a spat and we would end up spending the night in the car or the coal shed. So I just did a bit of Titania-style simpering, and kept my mouth shut.

Morning Glory looked at the paper in her hand again and read some more.

'Monday: This morning I woke fearing the magic might have vanished and I'd be back to my same old dull grey plodding self. But, no! Again today I seemed to walk on air. The mice scurried as I strode with heart aloft between the dark walls of this place. I think they sensed my growing confidence.'

She turned to Tristram. 'See?' she said. 'Unlike yourself, your nephew has a heart.'

'Pity he doesn't have a brain,' said Uncle Tristram.

Morning Glory read on. *'Tuesday: I've seen an angel! Speak to me last week and I would have told you she was nothing more than a pretty young lady. But I see more clearly now. She is a shining angel! I want to shout to those around me, "Look at her! Don't you see her radiance?" But I know better than to spill my secret. So I said nothing.'*

Morning Glory turned to me. 'You saw her, then! Up on the hill, you saw my angel Dido!'

'Maybe he didn't,' Uncle Tristram said, trying to make mischief. 'Maybe with all that radiant angel stuff, he's really talking about *you*.'

All right, then. So I *blushed*. But anybody would have blushed. It doesn't mean a thing. Except that Morning Glory leaned across and whispered, '*Was* it me you meant? You can say! I promise I won't tell.'

I snatched the holiday homework out of her hand and left the room. The last thing I heard as I ran up the stairs was Uncle Tristram sniggering.

FUNNY, THAT

I can't work out what woke me in the middle of the night. It might have been the rain, but after two full days and nights of water tippling down, you'd think that I'd have been accustomed to that.

Opening my eyes, I saw, behind rain-stippled

panes, the jet-black silhouette of the hill looming outside my window.

Funny, that. Because it hadn't been there the night before. Or the night before that. Or any night since we'd arrived. I'd lain in bed and seen a lot of things. I'd watched clouds billowing across the sky. I'd seen the dawn one morning. I'd seen a host of seagulls and more than one helicopter. I had seen thousands of raindrops scudding down the windowpanes.

But I had never seen the top of the hill.

Either the hill was getting higher, or this side of the house was sinking fast. *And* on a tilt.

I can't believe I just went back to sleep.

Saturday

THE LURE OF THE PORK PIE

I came downstairs to find Uncle Tristram frantically sweeping water out of the kitchen door. It was a losing battle. There was a flood all down the hall and in the living room.

'You find another broom,' he ordered me. 'We're getting *swamped* in here.'

'That isn't going to work.'

He glared at me. 'Have you a better idea?'

'Yes,' I said, and I walked down the hall to open the front door. All of the water went rushing that way.

'This house is now on a slope,' I said. 'And that end's *down*.'

We watched as the living room and kitchen gradually emptied. Soon there was just a stream of water pouring in at the back door, straight down the hall, and out the front.

We heard soft footfalls and looked up to see Morning Glory wrapped in a luminous rainbow poncho and wearing diamanté slippers. She leaned over the banisters. 'Heavens!' she said.

'Look at it! It's almost exactly like having a stream running through your house!'

'I hate to break this to you,' Uncle Tristram said. 'But that is exactly what it is.'

'What?'

'A stream running through your house.'

She thought for a moment, then her face crumpled. 'But what am I going to *do*?'

I only had one suggestion and that was feeble. 'Wait till it stops raining?'

Uncle Tristram was made of sterner stuff. 'Ignore this stream,' he urged her. 'Treat it with the contempt it deserves until it goes away.'

'What? Just step over it?'

'Or, if you choose, wade through. But don't for a moment let it cramp your style.'

'You might want to take off those rather pretty diamanté slippers,' I suggested. 'In case the sparkles rust. And if you want to make that fortune in London, you might be wise to rescue Aunty Audrey's clothes before those bags split and they all get soaked.'

Cheered, Morning Glory reached down to ease the diamanté slippers off her feet. Tossing them to Uncle Tristram, she stepped in the water. Together we rescued all the massive plastic bags and stowed them safely in the boot of Uncle Tristram's car. Then we waded upstream to the kitchen.

'No pork pies left, I suppose?' I asked, without much hope.

'Don't worry,' Uncle Tristram tried to console

me. 'I'll buy you a pork pie on a stick as soon as we get to the fair.'

'We're not still going?'

'Why on earth not?' He took in our astonished looks. 'Think of it this way,' he urged. 'All Morning Glory's happiness is at stake. She can't stand Officer Watkins up again. This time, he'd dump her for good. And I can't for the life of me think what we can do that's useful here, unless one of us turns out to be a secret star at building the sort of dams that can re-route a hill stream.'

Building the sort of dams that can re-route a hill stream . . .

Whoops!

There was a long, long silence.

Yes, yes! I know. I made the wrong decision! I failed the moral test. I should have leaped to my feet and cried, 'Of course! I know what caused this problem and I can solve it! I will miss coming to the fair, and my big chance to eat things on sticks! I will climb up that steep and soggy hill and unblock my dam. The stream will instantly go back to running down the other side, and you won't have this problem.'

Call it a craven nature. Call it the lure of the pork pie. But I said nothing.

TERMITES AND GAS
EXPLOSIONS AND AIRCRAFT
FALLING OUT OF THE SKY

Uncle Tristram tugged the tarpaulin off the top of the car and threw it on top of the plastic bags in the boot with a shudder. 'Disgusting! Completely bespattered with seagull poo. It looks more like camouflage than canvas.' He called to Morning Glory. 'Hurry up! We have a lot of things to munch through if we're to win this competition.'

She was still staring back over the fence. 'Is it my imagination,' she asked us suddenly, 'or is the house on a tilt?'

'A tilt?'

'You know. *Leaning*.'

It was my second chance to come clean. And I blew this one, too. 'It's obviously leaning a *tiny* bit,' I tried to soothe her, 'or the water wouldn't rush through. It would stay put, like lakes do. But it is, after all, a very old house.'

'Yes,' Uncle Tristram backed me up. 'I expect that getting the odd stream taking to coming in one door of your house and rushing out of the other is an entirely normal and quite common result of years of mild subsidence. Nothing to worry about at all. Just hop in the car, and we'll be off to the fair.'

He never should have mentioned 'subsidence'.

'Hang on a minute,' Morning Glory said. 'I'm sure I saw that word in Aunty Audrey's insurance policy. Perhaps there'll be something in there about streams running through your house as well.'

'Bound to be,' Uncle Tristram tried to assure her. He was getting impatient. 'Streams, rivers, brooks, burns, geysers, hot springs, mountain torrents – all *bound* to be adequately covered.'

'I think I'll just check.' Already she was taking off her diamanté slippers. He tried to grab her, but in a moment she was out of the car and picking her way back barefoot through the mud towards the house.

'We're going to be so *late*,' wailed Uncle Tristram.

'Look on the bright side. We'll be even hungrier.'

He cheered up. 'I could *murder* a chipolata on a stick.'

I took the chance of Morning Glory being gone to climb in the front seat. I half expected Uncle Tristram to order me back, but I suppose he thought that since she wasn't his girlfriend any more, he might as well not bother.

'Where *is* she?' Uncle Tristram kept grumbling, while I just thought about pork pies.

Finally she came back looking a bit dishevelled and clutching the envelope she had gone to fetch. 'Sorry! The stream's quite deep now. I had to take off all my clothes before I waded through.'

'You should have called!' insisted Uncle Tristram. 'I would have come to help you *in a flash.*'

We took off down the track. Morning Glory's face became more and more anxious as she read through the sections of the policy.

'Problem?' I asked her.

She shook her head. 'I don't know. I can't work it out at all.' She ran her finger down the page. 'I mean, it seems the house is fully covered for earthquake or fire, or even terrorist outrage.'

'If you want fire, go for young Harry here,'

131

urged Uncle Tristram. 'He is our family expert.'

Morning Glory ignored him. 'And you can have flood, or major or minor subsidence. You can have vandalism. It seems you can even have termites!' Her finger was still moving down the page. 'According to this, you can have gas explosions. And aircraft falling out of the sky (military or commercial).' She laid the policy down in her lap. 'But there is nothing – nothing at all – about streams running through your house.'

'Well, never mind,' said Uncle Tristram.

'We should go back,' insisted Morning Glory. 'If I'm not even *insured*, I really ought to try to barricade the door.'

'If you can barely even wade through the stream,' said Uncle Tristram, 'you won't be able to shut the door on it.' He went all cunning. 'Why don't we just press on? Then Officer Watkins won't get cross with you all over again for standing him up at a grand island social occasion, and you can ask his advice.'

'There's no point in getting his advice,' said Morning Glory, 'if I'm so far away from home that I can't take it.'

'Why can't he drive you back?'

'He doesn't have the squad car.' Morning

Glory pouted. 'Not on a Saturday. There's only one police car on the island, and Delia gets it on Saturday even if she's not fetching the chips.'

'Why don't I lend him this one?'

'Would you?' She turned to Uncle Tristram, radiant. 'You wouldn't mind?'

'Why should I?' Uncle Tristram asked. 'I shall be busy eating things on sticks.'

GAME PLAN

On the drive over the island, Uncle Tristram and I discussed our game plans.

'I'm going to set down a heavy meat base,' Uncle Tristram said. 'You know. Start with the steak on a stick, then the hot dog and then the meatball. Move through the pork pie and the salami until I reach the fishcake. Perhaps at that point I'll refresh the palate with the pickle on a stick. And then I plan to move in for what you might term the heavier desserts: the toffee apple on a stick, the frozen banana with sprinkles – finishing up with the ice lolly, the cheese puff and the candy floss.'

'That's mad,' I told him. 'You'll feel totally stuffed before you're even halfway through.'

'Oh, yes?' he huffed. 'So how are you planning to go about it?'

'I'm going to have my pork pie first,' I explained. 'Because that's breakfast, and you should never start the day without a good breakfast. And after that I'm moving on to the cheese puff because that's mostly puff. Then candy floss. That collapses into nothing. Pickles are vegetables, so they don't count. They barely line your stomach. I'll have the ice lolly on a stick next, I think, because that's nothing more than coloured water. So by the time I get round to any of the heavy stuff, I'll still be practically *starving*.'

Morning Glory leaned forward. 'Would you two mind?' she said. 'You're making me feel rather *sick*.'

We sat there quietly for a while. Then Uncle Tristram had a thought. 'Oh, by the way, I meant to ask you, Morning Glory. Who were those people your boyfriend was searching for when he went round the house?'

'Kidnappers.'

'*Kidnappers?*'

'Of that missing boy.' Morning Glory leaned

134

forward again. 'It seems he was away from home with some other member of his family, and both of them vanished. His parents have had a couple of anguished phone calls about him being kept in a cell and needing ransom money. Both of the calls were cut off before the police could trace the number. But he did manage to tell his mother just enough for them to work out he might be on this island.' She gave a little shiver. 'It's quite exciting, really – for round here, anyway.'

I felt a stirring of unease, just as I had when I first saw the stream running down the wrong side of the hill. 'So what does this missing boy look like?'

'The same as everyone you see on the telly,' Morning Glory said. 'Fuzzy grey blob.'

'And this relation of his? Fuzzy grey blob as well?'

'That's right!'

I tried a different tack. 'But why did the police think that he might be hidden in *your* house?'

'They didn't,' Morning Glory said. 'They have been looking everywhere. For days. It's just that Tom left searching my house till last because he was in such a sulk about my missing the dance, and didn't want to see me.'

'So this boy – he's still missing?'

'They're both still missing. But the police suspect the other fellow is dead.'

I glanced at Uncle Tristram. 'Dead? Why?'

'Because nobody's heard a word from him. And his mobile phone went off for good nearly a week ago.'

My feelings of unease were strengthening by the minute.

'Does that explain the helicopters?' Uncle Tristram asked.

'Yes,' Morning Glory said. 'They're looking for a yellow-topped car.'

There was a silence, though I could swear that I could hear Uncle Tristram's brain whirring away at full speed. After a moment I glanced his way again, to find that, this time, he was looking my way.

I can't explain what happened next. I mean, at any other time I know that one or the other of us would have come out with the words, 'You don't for a single moment suppose . . . ?'

But we had both of us had a horrible week. It had been raining for days. We had been eating weeds. Poor Uncle Tristram had lost Morning Glory back to her boyfriend. I'd been so bored

I'd even started on my holiday homework. Even the Battle of the Owls and Pigs had been a bit of a let-down.

Now here we were, less than ten minutes away from our only chance of having one good laugh (and a pork pie) before we left the island. We couldn't get home sooner anyway. The ferry didn't leave till six. We'd still be home tomorrow.

Still – Mum and Dad! I knew they must be mad with worry.

I sighed. 'Uncle Tristram, I really think you're going to have to stop at the next phone.'

He tried to hide his groan. 'Yes, I suppose I must.'

But as we drove along, we both had time to think. And perhaps it was the simple magic attraction of eating things on sticks, but by the time we came across a phone by the side of the road, we'd clearly hatched the very same idea.

'Now keep it brief!' he warned. 'No more than a few seconds at *most*. If anyone attempts to ensnare you in conversation, pretend you can't hear a thing. Simply repeat that we're both safe and well and will be home tomorrow. And then *hang up*.' So Morning Glory wouldn't get suspicious, he added vaguely, 'After all, we don't want to be late at the fair.' He scoured the sky anxiously for helicopters. 'And while you're doing that, I might just pull that old tarpaulin back over the top of the car.'

'Top plan,' I said. And so that Morning Glory would think nothing of it, I added, 'The seagull poo is really bad on this side of the island.'

A REAL OLD FOX STOLE WITH TEETH

We gazed around the fairground. Between the faded tents there were a few drab-looking trestle tables and battered food stands. Their signs were curling with age and peeling with damp, and made a rather good guessing game:

> ## IPOLATA ON A STI
> Buy your anan on a ck here.

That sort of thing.

The beards were out in force. Mr Appelini's goatee was being whipped upwards by the wind. George gave me a look of the deepest suspicion through his great mass of I'm-a-mad-prophet beard, and clapped his hands over his trouser pockets as if he thought I might be an excellent pickpocket as well as a skilled arsonist. I thought at first that one of the attractions was a gorilla, but it turned out to be Old Joe, resting on an upturned bucket. Ted Hanley's yew hedge-style beard must have grown even wider since we last saw him. Certainly everyone seemed to step hastily aside as he walked past them.

At the far end of the fairground there was a brand-new gleaming sign that sported every word in full.

> ## GRAND NEW BEST BEARD ON THE ISLAND COMPETITION

'So *that's* why they've all showed up!' said Uncle Tristram. 'What is the prize?'

'I'll go across and ask.' Pulling her luminous rainbow poncho closer around her black leather bodice, Morning Glory brushed down her pink tutu skirt and picked her way through the puddles towards the trestle table in her diamanté slippers.

A ripple of excitement ran through a group of people standing close by. Suddenly one of them rushed over and stopped Morning Glory in her tracks by seizing her hand and pumping it up and down.

'Congratulations! Oh, very well done! Excellent!'

Morning Glory looked a bit baffled.

The other people in the group were catching up now. 'Yes, very well done! Brilliant! You've won again, Morning Glory!'

'Won what?' I asked Uncle Tristram.

He jerked a thumb towards a sign propped up against another of the tables.

!BACK BY DEMAND: BEST DRESS-UP COMPETITION!

In my opinion, Morning Glory was very

140

gracious about it. She didn't tell them she had won again simply by wearing the clothes she had put on that morning. She accepted her prize – it was a real old fox stole with teeth – with a curtsey that would have done credit to Titania. She didn't even slip away to the adjoining field to dig a hole and bury the poor fox in harmony with the universe until the judges had all wandered off.

Uncle Tristram and I drew closer to the Best Beard Competition trestle table. 'Now, Harry,' Uncle Tristram warned. 'We must avert suspicion. So when we speak to people, do try your very, very hardest not to look like a fuzzy grey blob.'

As we approached, the man sitting behind the table looked up and inspected us gravely.

'Frankly,' he said, 'I don't think either of you should bother to enter. I very much doubt if you'll win.'

'We only wanted to know what you were offering as a prize,' said Uncle Tristram.

'It is a nit comb,' the man said proudly.

'A *nit* comb?'

'They're very useful,' said the man. 'And this one's made from a rather attractive mock tortoiseshell.'

'Still,' Uncle Tristram said, 'it isn't a prize you'd want to flash around much, is it? A *nit* comb.'

And shrugging his shoulders, he took off to get in line for our own competition, the Eating Things on Sticks.

HONOUR UNRIVALLED!

The rules were pretty strict. First, we were herded into a tent to have our photos taken.

'Why?' Uncle Tristram asked.

The bearded lady at the check-in table explained. 'To stop you cheating. You have to find a warden to watch you eat your things on sticks. They take your entry card from you, check your face matches the photograph as you are eating, and when you've swallowed the last of whatever it is, they tick it off your list and put their signature beside it.'

'All a bit *complicated*,' complained Uncle Tristram. 'I was just fancying eating a few things on sticks.'

I took a look at the list printed inside my card. There they all were: pork pie, hot dog, salami, ice lolly . . . I counted twenty-four. I couldn't *wait* to get started. 'How do you recognize a warden?'

'They're in the yellow jackets.'

I peered out through the tent flap. And sure enough, there did seem to be a good few men and women in yellow jackets milling about the fairground. Just as I turned back, out of the corner of my eye I saw the gable ends of a beard I thought I recognized passing the entrance to the tent.

I nudged Uncle Tristram's arm. 'Hey! Look over there. Isn't that Morning Glory's father?'

He glanced across. But whatever I'd seen had vanished.

'Can't see him myself.'

I shrugged. 'Oh, well. Probably just a shadow.' A rubber stamp came down on my hand to distract me. 'Ouch!' My hand glowed purple. 'What's all that about?'

'That's so you can't sneak out of the grounds,' said the official who had branded me. She brought the purple ink stamp down on Uncle Tristram's hand just as he asked her, mystified, 'Why would we want to sneak away from the fair if we are busy eating things on sticks?'

143

'In order to be sick,' said the official.

'That is *disgusting*.' Uncle Tristram shuddered and turned to the other entrants to ask rhetorically, 'Do they hang cameras in the lavatories as well?'

I noticed nobody piped up to say they didn't.

'It's all a bit *formal*, don't you think?' asked Uncle Tristram. 'All these rules. Just for a simple good fun blow-out?'

Everyone gasped.

'It's not just a simple blow-out!' the man beside us protested. He spoke so forcefully his silken beard lifted like a net curtain in a draught. 'There is a lot at stake!'

'What?' Uncle Tristram challenged. 'What's the prize?'

'Didn't you know? It's a whole week on the mainland.' His face went dreamy. 'Just imagine! Supermarkets! Cinemas! Banks! A choice of restaurants!'

'Trees!' I suggested.

'We have a tree on the island.'

We didn't tell him the bad news.

'What I don't understand,' said Uncle Tristram, 'is that there's such a splendid prize for winning Eating Things on Sticks. Yet all you get for being the Best Beard on the

Island is one measly nit comb.'

Everyone round us gasped again. Some even shrank back in horror.

'*All?*'

'*All* you get?'

'Did he say, "All you get is one measly nit comb"?'

Uncle Tristram determinedly stood his ground. 'Yes,' he said. 'One measly nit comb.'

Everyone looked to the man with the silken beard to put us right again.

'It isn't just the *nit* comb,' he explained. 'Enchanting as that is. It is the *honour*. Honour unrivalled!' He spread his hands. 'Think of it! Best Beard on the Island! And not just *any* old island. Here! Here where there were no razor blades at all during the Fifty Year Skirmish. Here where there was a scissor shortage during the Nine Year Ferry Strike. Here, where the Great Shaving Cream Shortage lasted for almost a decade. *Surely* you can imagine the sheer undiluted glory of being crowned the Best

Beard on this Island? Why it will be more of an honour even than – than . . . '

He waved a hand, as though scouring the air around us for the perfect example. Again, moving along the back of the tent wall, I saw that shadow of what looked like an exploding haystack.

'Than winning the Olympics?' I offered tentatively.

'Oh, at least! At *least*.'

As the man said these words, the shadow of what looked like an exploding haystack stopped dead behind the tent wall. It was such a *strange* silhouette that I was tempted to step out of line to track down its source. But we'd been waiting for so long already, I didn't want to risk losing my place.

It was another ten minutes before the check-in lady at the trestle table announced that everyone was stamped and photographed, and we were ready. 'Off you go!'

We all spilled out of the tent. 'Where's Morning Glory now?' demanded Uncle Tristram. 'It can't have taken her all this time to give one little fox stole a decent and harmonious funeral.'

I looked across the fairground. In the far corner, Morning Glory was about as close as

146

you can get to a police officer who is supposed to be busy doing his duty. They had their backs to us, and they were staring at a cottage that had a FOR SALE sign leaning against its wall.

I pointed. 'There they are.'

Uncle Tristram scowled. 'I certainly don't intend to miss that ferry this evening. So if they're going to borrow my car to go back and barricade that stream, they'd better get on with it.'

Almost as if she'd heard him all the way across the fairground, Morning Glory turned. She took Officer Watkins' arm and, pausing only once to blow a kiss back over her shoulder at the pretty little cottage, she led him off towards the car park.

Uncle Tristram lifted anxious eyes to the helicopters circling above us. 'I certainly hope he doesn't take off the tarpaulin.'

'Those helicopters won't be up there long,' I said. 'Mum's bound to tell them it's all been a terrible mistake.'

'You're sure you didn't spend too long explaining?'

'No, no,' I told him. 'Under ten seconds.'

'Good lad. We should be safe then.' He turned to face me and stuck out his hand.

147

'Right,' he said. 'Though we may stroll together amiably through this great wonderland of things on sticks, we are as though sworn enemies with daggers drawn. In your own time! And may the toughest stomach win!'

EATING THINGS ON STICKS

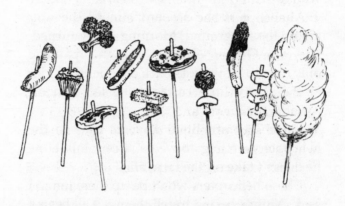

We had a grand time after that. The rain made some things taste a little slimy and turned some others soggy. I must admit my candyfloss was positively pitted. But you can't ruin pork pie on a stick. Or sausage. Toffee apple on a stick holds up quite well against the occasional downpour.

I had a bit of a run-in with one of the wardens when half my fishfinger broke away and fell in a puddle. She thought I ought to start over again with a fresh one. But Uncle Tristram argued my case quite forcefully – not wanting to pay for it – and in the end she did give up and tick my card.

An hour later, while I was tipping back my head to catch the drippings from the ice lolly on a stick that I'd forgotten to eat earlier, I noticed the helicopters had stopped circling. I swung round to see them heading for the mainland – a little line of beetles across the sky.

'Mum's told them we're all right, then.'

'Good,' Uncle Tristram said. He shivered. 'You realize you and I are going to get a frightful slice of tongue pie from your mother when we get back.'

'I know.' I was distracted from my own short ripple of fear by a disturbance around us. Everyone began to whisper.

'It's Delia! Delia's coming!'

'Look! Look! She's walking *this* way.'

Excitement was intense. 'See? Delia's coming! Everyone make way for Delia!'

The crowds fell back, to make a sort of avenue of beards. Into sight stepped a police officer. She was tall and slim. She wore her sleek black uniform as proudly as if she were a general on parade. And she was eating chips.

I nudged Uncle Tristram. '*There's* one that they've forgotten. Chips on a stick!'

He didn't answer. I glanced up at him. He wasn't even listening. Just like the beardies, he was staring straight ahead at Delia as if a shining angel were passing by.

I poked him hard. 'No! Don't even *think* of it!'

'She's very beautiful,' he whispered. A dreamy look spread over his face. 'And look at what she's wearing! Isn't that *fantastic*? So simple and so smart. So sober and so black.'

'Stop it!' I shook him. 'Stop it at once! She lives here, don't forget. And you are never, ever to fall in love again with anyone who lives on this island!'

It was as if I'd said the exact right words to break the spell. The dreamy look passed from his face.

'You're right,' he said, and gazed around us. 'So what do you reckon? Where shall we go next? Steak on a stick? Or are you still on the desserts?'

MY LONG-LOST COUSIN

We were just heading for the frozen banana on a stick stand when Uncle Tristram nudged me.

I looked up from my chipolata. 'What?'

'Look over there.' He jerked a thumb towards the car park. 'See what I see?'

I peered across. There, scrambling out of Uncle Tristram's car, was Morning Glory. Tugging his uniform straight, Officer Watkins climbed out after her.

'He must drive very fast,' I said, 'for them to have got back this soon.'

'I don't think they've been anywhere at all!' said Uncle Tristram. 'The whole car's totally steamed up.' A little bitterly he added, 'Being in the presence of the old boyfriend has clearly turned out to be a whole lot more exciting than being in the presence of an apple.'

I tried to cheer him up. 'I expect she'll make him sit cross-legged in the mud and thank his lips now.'

But Uncle Tristram was still a bit put out at being trumped in love. He glowered as Morning Glory and Officer Watkins came over

151

towards us. 'Been very *busy*, have you both?' he asked sarcastically. 'Spent all this time desperately barricading Aunt Audrey's back door against the torrent?'

Morning Glory did at least have the grace to blush. But Officer Watkins grinned. 'We didn't go. We just sat in your car—'

'So I see,' Uncle Tristram said, horribly frostily.

'– and agreed to get married!' He stuck his hand out. 'And Morning Glory wanted you to be the first to know – since you're her long-lost second cousin twice removed.'

That startled Uncle Tristram. '*Am* I?'

Morning Glory let out a tinkling laugh and shook a warning finger at Uncle Tristram. 'Don't be so silly,' she scolded. 'You know you are! And Harry here is yet another long-lost cousin. It was so good of dear Aunt Susan to bring us together after all these long-lost years.'

I was so glad not to have to be Titania, I didn't mind whose long-lost cousin I became. So I gave Morning Glory a giant hug. 'Congratulations, cuz!'

She turned to Uncle Tristram. In a spot, he had to hug her, too. Then, after a moment's slightly peeved consideration, he turned to Officer Watkins and shook hands with him as well. 'Oh, all right. Congratulations to you both.' He stood there for a moment longer, then simply added, 'Right, then. Now that we're all successfully in harmony with the universe, I might go back to my pork pie on a stick.'

Morning Glory ignored him. 'We're not just getting *married*,' she pressed on happily. She pointed to the FOR SALE sign. 'We're going buy that house as soon as I've managed to sell Aunty Audrey's.'

'Better get back and have that go at barricading the stream, then,' said Uncle Tristram.

'Yes,' she agreed. 'So are you ready?'

We stared. 'Who, us?'

She smiled seraphically. 'Of course. For one thing, I'll need all the help that I can get. And for another, it's not as if you're doing anything important here.'

'We are,' I said. 'We're trying to win the Eating Things on Sticks prize.'

'But *why*?' She spread her hands. 'The only thing you'll win is what you'll have tomorrow anyway. A whole week on the mainland. The only thing you're doing here is putting yourselves totally out of harmony with the universe by stuffing yourselves with quite disgusting foodstuffs that will make you sick.'

I was already feeling a tiny bit queasy. But when she said that, I felt worse. I held my chipolata on a stick a little further away from me, and turned to Uncle Tristram. 'She is right, you know.'

'Yes,' Uncle Tristram said. 'I know she's right. It's just that I'd prefer to spend my very last afternoon on this island walking round eating things on sticks to being in a cold and miserable house mopping up water.'

'Oh, come on,' Morning Glory said. 'Fair's fair, Tristram. You owe me one small favour. You've had a lovely, *lovely* week at my house. You've even seen an angel!'

The dreamy smile came back on Uncle Tristram's face. 'Well, there is that,' he found himself conceding. 'I've seen an angel.'

He set off cheerily through the gathering crowd towards the car park, singing a song in which the words 'Beautiful Delia, Queen of my Heart' featured enough to get on my nerves and irritate Morning Glory intensely.

THE BEST BEARD
ON THE ISLAND

'Make way! Excuse me! Could we please get through! We're in a bit of a hurry here!'

The crowd weren't budging, even for Officer Watkins.

'What's going on?' I asked.

'I don't know.' Uncle Tristram shrugged. 'Maybe it's jugglers. Or a magician or something.'

Fat chance, I thought. And I was right. When we had shoved our way far enough through the crowd to see what everyone was staring at, it was the beards.

'Don't stop,' said Uncle Tristram. 'Keep pushing through.'

But Officer Watkins had come to a halt. 'Hey, Morning Glory. Isn't that—? Up there on the platform. Look! Surely . . . ?'

He stared. She stared. We all stared. Morning Glory let out a gasp of astonishment. '*Dad* . . . ?'

And yes, indeed. It was her father standing there, holding a placard that said quite plainly: ENTRANT NO. 17.

'I simply don't *believe* it,' Uncle Tristram said.

'What is that miserable old body doing here? The man as good as *promised* he would be spending the whole of today in bed with his face to the wall.'

I turned to Morning Glory. Her faintest flush of pink was deepening by the moment. Raising her arms, she waved to him frantically above the heads of the crowd. 'Oh, good luck, Dad! Good luck!'

I didn't see how anyone whose head was swathed in such an unruly snap! crackle! pop! of hair could possibly hear well enough to catch this cry of encouragement. So I was not surprised to see him turn the other way. But then I realized that was not because he hadn't heard the cry from Morning Glory. It was because he was already listening to someone else. There, on the other side of the semi-circle of people admiring the eight grand finalists of the Best Beard competition, there was a woman wearing a sparkly purple shift, lace mittens and pixie boots, waving a brolly which had flashing lights.

Who else but Morning Glory's mother?

'Good luck!' she was shouting cheerily. 'Oh, best of luck! I really hope you win! You certainly deserve the prize!'

And then there was the strangest miracle.

Morning Glory's father smiled.

Yes, Mr McFee smiled! I'm not sure how we knew. Perhaps some of the wispy bits of his mad beard were lifted somehow in the breeze. But there was no disputing it. He gave a radiant smile.

That was the moment when the judges shuffled out of the tent. We stood in a breathless hush as they walked up and down in front of the finalists, studying in turn each goatee, silken avalanche and bushy beard. We waited with our hearts a-thump as they made notes on their clipboards. We sighed with anticipation as they retired behind the flaps of the tent to start their deliberations.

I could see Uncle Tristram glancing at his watch. Anxiety was plain on his face. Only a couple of hours now until the ferry left! But none of us could tear ourselves away. We had become a part of the crowd, desperate to hear the result. And by the time the judges finally came out again, we were all standing at the front, around Morning Glory.

'And the winner of the Best Beard Competition is . . .'

I honestly think that I came close to a heart attack.

'Mr McFee!'

Oh, the punches of triumph and cries of delight! The stamps and cheers of the crowd. The hoots of relief. The hugs of joy between Mr McFee and his wife.

'Oh, Albert!'
'Oh, Angeline!'
'Oh, Alby!'
'Oh, Angie!'
'Lambkin!'
'Sweetpea!'

They only tore themselves apart, with Mr McFee still beaming, for the Grand Prizegiving.

The mayor of the island gave a short speech. It all got muffled somewhere in his beard, but no one minded. Most of them just wandered off, chattering excitedly among themselves about the honour and unrivalled glory, and the rather nice mock-tortoiseshell nit comb. In the end, we were the only people left, and Uncle Tristram was getting more and more anxious. 'Really, we must press on. We have a door to barricade and a ferry to catch.'

'A ferry to catch?'

On Mr McFee, these words worked just like magic. Utterly galvanized, he pushed his daughter and Officer Watkins towards the car park. 'Quick, Morning Glory. Hurry along. Your friends mustn't miss the ferry! No one must ever miss a ferry again. So hurry along! Whatever it is you're barricading, go and do it now. Quick! Hurry! Hurry!'

AND THERE IT WASN'T

We took the last tight corner before you reach Aunty Audrey's house, and there it wasn't.

Yes, that's right. Wasn't.

There was the new stream, a whole lot wider than when we'd left that morning. Along its edges lay a sort of tidemark of old bricks, strands of coloured wool and little heaps of rubble. Quite a few heavy bits of furniture were still exactly where they'd been. But there was no house around them. Nothing stood higher than Aunt Audrey's wardrobe, which had clearly dropped as if from heaven and landed upright in the mud that Officer Watkins had been complaining about so bitterly earlier.

Morning Glory was devastated. 'What on earth's *happened?* Where on earth has it gone?'

'I think it's been swept away,' said Uncle Tristram.

'But it's a *house.*'

'Not any more, it isn't,' said Officer Watkins. He started prowling up and down the banks of the stream, looking for clues. The pangs of guilt that I'd been feeling on and off all day suddenly crystallized into decision.

'Excuse me,' I said. 'I will be back in a minute.'

I think they all suspected that, with the lavatory swept off downstream, I'd rushed to the undergrowth around the hill for quite a different purpose. I wasn't stopping to explain. I simply vanished between the bushes and hoped that, in the shock of things, they would forget me. Certainly, each time I looked down from wherever I'd reached on the climb up, they seemed still to be wandering about like shell-shocked soldiers.

On and on I climbed, higher and higher. At times the brand-new stream had taken over the old path so, slapped at by wet leaves and splattered by raindrops, I ploughed through the sodden wet undergrowth.

In the end, panting quite desperately, I reached the top.

The job did not take long. All I had to do was kick a few stones around. As if with relief – ah! that's a whole lot better! – the first few tricklings of the stream washed away all the mud I'd packed around the stones, and fell straight back into its old route down the other side. It was so quick and easy I felt even more guilty. Why hadn't I sneaked up and done it way back on Thursday, when I first realized? I could have saved the house!

I took a little more time coming down again. For one thing I used the old path, and since the last of the stream I had diverted that way by accident was only just dribbling away, it was quite slimy underfoot. And for another, I was in no hurry to get to the bottom and have to explain how this extraordinarily forceful stream had vanished.

They were all standing with their backs to me, staring at the tail end of the stream as it disappeared round the corner.

I shuffled up beside Uncle Tristram. He glared at me suspiciously, then took my arm and led me out of earshot. 'It's just this minute stopped,' he hissed at me. 'We've just been watching the last of it run past.' His eyes narrowed. 'Destroying houses is *your* speciality, isn't it? So what did you do up there to cause that stream in the first place?'

'Just kicked a few stones about,' I said vaguely.

'Just kicked a few stones about?' His eyes went wide. 'Just kicked a few stones about? You mean you made a *dam*? I don't believe it! While we were up there that day, you actually were daft enough to build a *dam*?'

'It wasn't a *real* dam. It was only *tiny*.'

'It didn't need to be anything *other* than tiny, right up there at the top!'

Hastily he stopped haranguing me as Morning Glory came rushing over towards us.

'You just missed something *amazing*,' she informed me. 'While you were up the hill, the stream just stopped. It just came to an end. It was a real, live miracle!'

I don't know what came over me, I really don't. 'Yes,' I said. 'I went up the hill and called the angels for help. I asked for Dido in particular. And Dido stopped it.'

Morning Glory clasped her hands together. 'Really?'

'Really,' I said.

'She came at once? And miracled away the stream?'

'I told Dido what had happened. And she just fixed it.'

Now Morning Glory was agog. '*How* did she fix it?'

'Probably just kicked a few stones about,' Uncle Tristram muttered.

I gave him one of those Watch-your-step-Buster looks that Mum gives me, and turned back to Morning Glory. 'She just did,' I said firmly. 'Using her special and angelic magic powers.'

Morning Glory looked quite ecstatic. Her eyes shone.

'Well that is wonderful! Perfectly *wonderful*! And now that the stream has been stopped, we will be able to . . . '

She faltered. Swinging around, she took in the bleak sight of a few damp lumps of giant furniture stuck in the mud with no walls at all around them.

'We will be able to . . . '

Her voice trailed to a halt.

'You can't *rebuild*,' said Uncle Tristram, valiantly trying to suppress his shudder of horror at the mere idea. He waved a hand at the few pitiful strands of coloured wool and bits of shattered debris lying around us. 'No, you must see it as a beautiful and vanished dream. A glorious old house, filled with old-fashioned charm and pretty little knick-knacks, and with the loveliest apple tree on the island.'

'It was the *only*—'

I jumped to avoid the hand that had shot out to swipe me.

'No!' Uncle Tristram persisted. 'You must do the sensible thing. Never look back! Set your face forward! Imagine your cosy future with Officer Watkins here in that divine little cottage beside the fairground. Think of the roses you will grow around your door. Think of the babies the two of you will soon be dandling on your knees. Take the insurance money.'

Morning Glory looked a bit startled. 'Will they pay out?'

'Of course they'll pay out,' said Uncle Tristram. 'Their only problem is going to be deciding under which of the many headings in the insurance policy you ought to claim.'

'I should think subsidence,' Officer Watkins said firmly. 'I think they're definitely going to decide to go for serious subsidence.'

'Flood, I'd say,' Uncle Tristram argued.

I thought I might as well put in my pennyworth. 'But by the time anyone comes in on next week's ferry to inspect the place, the ground around here will have dried out a bit, and they might decide that it looks more like a gas explosion. Or a terrorist outrage.'

'But there's no sign of blast or fire,' said Uncle Tristram. From his wide range of threatening looks, he shot me one of the darkest. 'Though I think we could safely say there have been signs of *vandalism*.'

I blushed, and shut up after that.

Morning Glory brushed all of their opinions aside. 'But I'll *explain*. I'll tell them exactly what happened. I'll tell them that all of a sudden, as if by magic, there was a stream that appeared completely out of nowhere, rushed down the mountainside and washed my house away.'

'I think they might find that a *little* hard to believe,' warned Uncle Tristram.

'No,' Morning Glory said. 'Because I'll go on to explain how the stream vanished. How this young boy–' She slid an affectionate arm around my shoulder. 'No, this young hero who was staying here all week climbed up the hill and asked my favourite angel to magic the stream away.'

She beamed around at all of us.

'And the angel did!'

There was a tiny little silence. Then Uncle Tristram rallied. 'Don't be *astonished*,' he said as gently as he could, 'if anyone who hears that thinks that you are just in shock because you no longer have a home.'

We heard a booming voice behind. 'Of course my precious daughter has a home!'

We all spun round. There, standing hand in hand, were Morning Glory's mother and father. He still appeared to be beaming. 'If Morning Glory needs a roof over her head until she's bought her new cottage, she can live with *us*.'

We watched him squeeze his wife's hand as he so happily said the word 'us', and Morning Glory's mother raised herself on tiptoe to kiss him through his storm of a beard.

After a moment he broke away as if an awful thought had suddenly occurred to him. Hastily glancing at his watch, he said to Uncle Tristram anxiously, 'Hadn't the two of you better get your skates on? If you're not careful you will miss that ferry!'

Home Again

PLERP LARP TENELLIN

I think I must be a martyr to seasickness.

'That,' Uncle Tristram said virtuously as he watched me heave quite a few things off sticks over the rails into the churning water, 'is probably because you didn't take Morning Glory's very good advice and make the effort to thank your stomach for doing all that extra work for you.'

A sudden swell beneath the ferry caused it to pitch and roll. Out of the corner of my eye I saw Uncle Tristram clutch his own stomach and turn the same green as the tea towel I'd set on fire on the grill.

'You don't look all that much in harmony with the universe yourself,' I snapped.

When we had both completely finished throwing up, we leaned together side by side at the bow.

'All in all,' Uncle Tristram said, his spirits visibly rising, 'that was a really good week. Lots of fresh air, and mucking about with mud, and dressing up and stuff.' He looked at me sternly. 'I certainly hope you enjoyed yourself even if you didn't manage to fit in your favourite pastime.'

'My favourite pastime?'

'Burning down kitchens. But you did at least get to totally destroy one house.'

I gave him a sour look. 'A pity Morning Glory didn't have a cat,' I said. 'You could have had a go at your own little speciality, and flattened it in some flower bed.'

He grinned, and we went back to keeping our eyes peeled for the mainland. At last the grey mist of horizon gathered itself into a darker line.

'There! See! Over there!'

'Thank heavens for that!'

We stood in silence, gazing at the approaching land. I know I was relieved to be on the way home. Still, I was anxious about the way they'd greet me. (Probably not with open arms and cries of 'Lambkin! You're back!') After all, Mum and Dad had just spent nearly a whole week of ghastly days and sleepless nights worrying themselves silly about me, and making tea for police negotiators waiting for my calls and technicians hoping to trace them. Five days in which a host of helicopter pilots had been scrambled to scour the island for any sign of Uncle Tristram's car. A week, frankly, after which, rather than stepping into the usual blizzard of welcoming hugs and kisses, you would expect me to walk through the door and get a rocket and my ears torn off.

Gradually the fuzzy grey line of coast began to look darker and sharper.

'Look!' Uncle Tristram dug his elbow in my ribs excitedly. 'I think I see a tree!'

The ferry forged in closer through the waves with Uncle Tristram leaning so keenly over the rails I had to keep hold of his jacket. After a while, he turned and said, 'Now, Harry, you'll admit that Morning Glory was a lovely-looking girl. And as for that Delia, she was an absolute *marvel*.' He pointed as the dock hove into view. 'But *that* – that is without a shadow of a doubt the most attractive sight that I have seen all week.'

Over the tannoy came a muffled announcement. 'Plerp larp tenellin!'

'Excellent!' said Uncle Tristram. And just as if he'd understood whatever it was the woman was saying though her beard, he led the way back down the steps so that, when the boat docked, we would be the very first ones off.

A WEIGHTED CANDLESTICK?
BARE HANDS?
A KITCHEN KNIFE?

Uncle Tristram switched off the engine before we even reached the gate and rolled the Maverati to a silent halt on top of the petunias.

'Let's hope they didn't get another cat while we were gone,' I said sarcastically.

He turned to give me a high-five. 'Well, there you go,' he said. 'Hop out.'

I stared in panic. 'Aren't you coming in?'

'Don't tell me you're too chicken to face the music by yourself.'

'Yes,' I admitted.

He sighed. 'Oh, all right. I do understand your terror. My sister is a fearsome creature when she's riled.' He winced at what I took to be one or two rather nasty childhood memories he didn't choose to share. 'I shall be brave and join you.'

He did unfasten his seat belt, but made no move to leave the safety of the car.

Neither did I.

After a few more silent and unmoving moments, he said to me, 'Perhaps what we need here is another game plan.'

'What's worrying me,' I said, 'is what I'm going to say when they start in with all their questions.'

'Just clutch your hand to your head,' he advised. 'Tell them you simply can't bear to talk about it. Say it just brings back nightmares.'

'And what about when the police show up to hand in their bill for a week's worth of telephone tapping?'

'You made those calls in all good faith,' he said.

'And when the Combined Air Services demand compensation for all those extra and unnecessary helicopters?'

'Excellent practice for our armed forces. They should be *grateful*.' He spread his hands like someone pleading innocence in the dock. 'After all, Harry, it isn't as if we have told any *lies*. I think that we can safely claim that we are still in harmony with the universe.'

'I think we'll be even more in harmony with the universe in a minute,' I told him glumly. 'In fact, I rather suspect that, in a few minutes, you and I will very probably both be *dead*.'

We sat in silence for a little while till Uncle Tristram got bored enough to say, 'Oh, well then. No real point in putting it off.'

'No,' I said dubiously.

'So shall we go and see which murder weapon your mother has decided to use? A weighted candlestick? Bare hands? A kitchen knife?'

'Yes, let's.'

We both got out of the car. I noticed that neither of us spoke, or slammed our door, and both of us picked our way as softly as we could over the few unsquashed petunias between the front wheels of the car and the front porch.

I slid my key in the door and turned it quietly. We crept into the hall. I could hear voices coming from the television in the living room so, looking for any old excuse to put off the dreadful moment, I pushed at the kitchen door.

Ta-*ra*! It opened on a gorgeous room with gleaming cabinets and shiny tops and magic pools of light pouring from nowhere. Honestly, it looked *fantastic*. The walls were pristine and the cupboard doors the richest, deepest scarlet. The bright new cover on the brand-new ironing board bore not a single scorch mark.

'Hey!' Uncle Tristram whispered. 'New freezer! Handsome!'

'Look at that oven hob! Ace-matic!'

'I like the new blinds.'

I stepped back. 'Seen the floor tiles?'

'Groovy! I reckon you've done your family a giant favour, Harry. This is a huge improvement on before. Look at that space-age microwave.'

I spun round. 'Where?'

'Built in. There. See?'

He pointed. That was his mistake. I merely followed the direction of his finger and there it was. The brand-new microwave. And when, by sheer force of habit, I found myself reaching out to press *Defrost – One Minute*, not expecting anything at all to happen, this supersonic clean machine with snow-white buttons actually obeyed at once.

'Whoops! Sorry.'

I turned back to see Uncle Tristram staring at me in horror. 'Oh, well done!' he hissed. 'That should cut both our life expectancies right down to fifty-seven seconds at most. Can't you *cancel* the blasted thing?'

'I could,' I said. 'But if it's like our last one, it'll make exactly the same noise. But even sooner.'

He shrugged. 'Oh, well. I suppose it had to happen sometime. Might as well get it all over with.'

I panicked. '*You're* all right. You don't live here. But I am going to get *mashed*. I reckon it'll be so bad I'll end up begging to come back to you.'

He scowled. 'Well, don't think I'll be taking you on any more trips. I've had enough of holidays. Next time, we're going to stay home.'

Tipping his head back suddenly, he shut his eyes. 'Yes! That's the plan for next time. Stay in the city. Bliss! Utter bliss! Think of it, Harry! When we get hungry, we can shop in supermarkets or eat in restaurants. When we get bored, we won't have to traipse up and down windy beaches, being pooed on by seagulls. We can go to the cinema, or swim in pools with flumes . . .'

It sounded so tempting, my worries all began to fade.

Uncle Tristram still looked ecstatic. 'When we run out of money, I can simply go to a cash machine or step into the nearest bank. If we watch television, everyone on it will have proper heads and not just fuzzy grey blobs.'

Feeling a little more in harmony with the universe myself, I punched the air and whispered, 'Yes!' just as the microwave went:

Ping!

Uncle Tristram broke off. 'Well,' he reproved me. 'That should be loud enough to bring the wolves down on the fold.'

We waited. And we waited.

I crossed my fingers as the footsteps crossed the hall.

The door flew open. There my parents stood.

HOME AND DRY

I don't have to go into sordid detail, do I? I mean, you must have been through this sort of thing yourself. You'll know the score. I don't have to list all of their 'How *could* you . . . ?'s, and their 'Why in heaven's name didn't you . . . ?'s, and their 'Surely it must have *occurred* to you that . . . !'s, and their 'How do you think we . . . ?'s, and their 'I simply can't *believe* . . . !'s. It went on for ages. Absolutely ages. I was exhausted at the end.

We gave as good as we got. Uncle Tristram was brilliant with all his 'How on earth were we supposed to know . . . ?'s, and his 'Why should we for a single *moment* think . . . ?'s, and his 'You're being quite unreasonable . . . !'s, and his 'It's not as if we were deliberately . . .'s.

I backed him up. I came out fighting with my own 'It isn't *our* fault that . . . !'s, and my 'Nobody *told* us . . . !'s, and my 'You never *said* I had to . . . !'s, and my 'Anyone else would have done the *same* . . . !'s, and my 'I don't know why you're blaming *me* . . . !'s.

In the end, everything calmed down a bit. Dad made some toast. Mum introduced a sour note by muttering, 'Please don't let Harry anywhere near the tea towels until that toaster's been unplugged at the mains.'

But I could tell the very worst was over.

Phew!

When Uncle Tristram was sure that we were pretty well home and dry, he reached for his jacket and car keys. 'Well, that's me ready for bed. Better be off.'

I followed him back through the petunias to the car. 'Thanks for the help.'

'No problem,' Uncle Tristram bragged. 'My sister doesn't frighten me.'

'She does.'

'Well, obviously,' he defended himself, 'when she is in one of her moods, even a Genetically Modified Giant Cockroach from the Planet Battle would take the long route round her.' To cover his embarrassment at having lied, he reached in the Maverati's boot to pull out my rucksack, and as he tugged away at it, one of the plastic bags that we had stuffed with Aunty Audrey's leftover clothes split down the side.

Out fell two pretty beaded purses.

'Here,' he said. 'Give your mum one of these.

She'll love it. Tell her it's a gift from your holidays. Then she can't change her mind and start to sulk at you again tomorrow.'

'She's not like that,' I said. 'And anyway, they're Morning Glory's purses, so she ought to get the money for both of them.'

He turned them over in his hand. 'I don't know,' he told me dubiously. 'Both of them look a bit tatty. They can't be worth much.' He thrust one at me. 'Go on, Harry. Take it. I promise that when I sell all this rubbish to the vintage clothing shop, I'll pay Morning Glory twice over for the other purse. You just tell Tansy it's from both of us. Then things will be fair all round.'

I couldn't think of any reason to argue. So I went back inside the house.

CLAIRETTE SHARD

Mum couldn't believe it. 'Harry! But this is vintage Clairette Shard! And apart from one or two loose beads that can be fixed, it's in pristine condition. It must be worth an absolute fortune! Where on earth did you find it?'

'More to the point,' my dad said, 'how much did Harry pay for it?'

Here is the proof that it's always better and safer not to tell lies. I came quite close to choosing what I thought a sensible amount – a couple of quid or so – and coming out with that.

Mercifully, Mum beat me to it. 'Whatever Harry paid, it can't be what it's worth. If you go into one of those vintage clothes shops, you find these Clairette Shard purses are selling for three thousand pounds.'

My mouth fell open. So did Dad's.

FURIOUS

Uncle Tristram was *furious*. 'Three thousand pounds? You should have simply snatched it back!'

I held the phone a little further away from my ear to try to protect myself. It seemed to me that for the last two hours I had been trying to defend myself from quite unreasonable attacks.

'How could I snatch it back? I'd only just that minute *given* it to her. "Here!" I'd just said. "This is a present to you from me and Uncle Tristram." Those were my very words. How could I snatch it back?'

'You should have tried!'

'It wouldn't have worked in any case. She was holding the thing as tightly as if it were a heap of crown jewels.'

'It practically *is* crown jewels!' he grumbled. 'Three thousand pounds! It's going to take me twenty years to pay back Morning Glory!'

The phone went silent for a while, and then he started up again. 'You should have snatched it back!'

He had been good to me that night. So even though I only wanted to go to bed, I made one last big effort. 'Look on the bright side,' I comforted him. 'It's very nice to think that Morning Glory will end up getting this sort of money for all that rubbish in the bags. And if we hadn't given this purse to Mum, you would have accepted any old stupid amount from the shop for the other one.'

'That's true enough,' he said. 'And probably for all the other stuff as well.'

I waited, yawning, while he thought it through, and in the end, as usual, came up with one of his plans. 'Listen to me, Harry. Tomorrow I'll bring back the bags. Tansy can go through them for me and tell me what each thing is worth. And in return, I'll let her keep the purse, and I'll explain to Morning Glory that she is quids in, really, because without your mum, I'd have accepted tuppence.'

185

'I think she'll think that's fair,' I said (though I was really far too tired to think about anything any more).

'Right, then,' said Uncle Tristram. 'A busy day tomorrow. Off you go to bed.'

GOOD HOLS?

Ralph was asleep. I woke him up by stumbling over his scout boots and falling on his bed.

'Oh, hey!' he said. 'Good hols?'

'Not bad,' I told him. 'How was scout camp?'

'Pretty good. We climbed a mountain.'

'So did we,' I said.

'We spent a bit of time in boats.'

'Yes, so did we.'

'It rained a lot.'

'Ditto.'

'My bed was damp.'

'Mine was as well.'

'The food was rubbish.'

'Can't have been any worse than ours.'

'Good company, though.'

'Yes,' I agreed. 'I had good company as well.'

'Well, he said. 'Your trip sounds more or less

the same as mine. So I might skip scout week and come along with you next time you burn down the kitchen.'

'You'd be most welcome,' I told him.

Then I fell asleep.

If you enjoyed this book, you might enjoy
reading another tale by Anne Fine about Harry
and his family. Read on for a few pages from
The More the Merrier –
a Christmas story.

'A wickedly seasonal tale' *The Times*

The More the Merrier

by Anne Fine

Christmas Eve

WRITING LETTERS TO SANTA

On Christmas Eve morning, everyone
arrived in their separate clumps, and there
was all the usual fuss about bagging the
best beds and warmest rooms. Great-
Granny wanted windows facing south. ('So
she can quarrel with the moon all night,'
Dad suggested.)

Then Great-Aunt Ida had to tell us all
about her 'twisted wrist'. ('That makes a
change,' said Mum. 'Usually it's a sprained
ankle so she can park in the comfiest chair
and not move for six days.')

After that, Titania had one of her

'sensitive' fits, saying she wouldn't be able to sleep in the room she'd been given because 'the wall has got stains in the shapes of ugly faces'.

'You ought to feel more at home, then,' Harry said.

He got sent to his room for that. So then, of course, I was the one who had to swap beds with Titania. (And *still* Mum claims Harry isn't her favourite.)

Then Aunt Susan dragged everyone out for a nature walk. (Harry got out of it by pretending he hadn't heard Mum say that he could come down again.) There is a limit to how exciting anyone can make the life history of a holly berry sound, so I wasn't really listening when she went on to mistletoe.

As soon as we'd got home again, Titania decided the next thing she wanted to do was write a letter to Santa. This is the sort of soppy idea that makes Aunt Susan clap her hands and say Titania is 'so uncynical'. (Dad calls it 'daft for her age'.)

'Oh, really. Not now,' Mum said. 'I'm about to set the table.'

But Aunt Susan gave her a look, and Mum

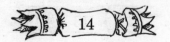

gave up, and agreed she could leave setting the table till later.

'Won't the boys join Titania?' asked Aunt Susan.

Harry snorted and left the room. I made to follow but Mum collared me. 'You'll stay, Ralph, won't you? Just to keep Titania company?'

'What, sit and write a betsy-wetsy letter to Santa? Are you joking?'

'Ssh!' Mum reproved me. 'Be polite.' (Which means, 'Don't scrap with me in front of visitors.')

Defeated, I slumped at the table. Aunt Susan gave me a few sheets of plain paper. Titania rushed upstairs to fetch her own out of her suitcase. (It was smelly and pink, and sprinkled with glitter.)

I wrote:

Dear Santa,

For Christmas, I would like a skunk, a real dead human skull, a Vespa PX125, a motorized glitter ball, a King of the Frogs poster, a ride in a hot-air balloon—

'Mummy!' called Titania. 'Ralph's being horribly, horribly greedy!'

— a Game Boy Advance, a flight in a Tiger Moth, a side of smoked salmon, a pair of Rocker GTS headphones, and a day white-water rafting down the Colorado river.

Titania wrote:

Dear, dear, lovely, sweet Mr Santa—

'Crawler!' I accused her.
'Mummy!' she called. 'Mum-mee! Ralph is calling me names!'
'Oh, get on with it,' I told her.
She got on with it.

16

ABOUT THE AUTHOR

ANNE FINE was born in Leicester. She went to Wallisdean County Primary School in Fareham, Hampshire and then to Northampton High School for Girls. She read Politics and History at the University of Warwick and then worked as an information officer for Oxfam before teaching (very briefly!) in a Scottish prison.

She started her first book during a blizzard that stopped her getting to Edinburgh City Library and has been writing ever since. She has won many awards for her books, has twice been voted Children's Writer of the Year at the British Book Awards and was the Children's Laureate for 2001–2003.

She lives in County Durham.

www.**annefine**.co.uk

aNNe FiNe

Frozen Billy

'I hate Frozen Billy – his painted, staring wooden eyes, the way his eyelids click when Uncle Len pulls a string, his long thin legs and his bright red wooden mouth . . .'

Clarrie and Will live with their Uncle Len – a brilliant ventriloquist in the nearby music hall. But Top Billing is out of Len's grasp until Will thinks up a way to double the drama with a new act and some extraordinary new patter that he and Frozen Billy can share on stage.

It's a grand idea. But to Clarrie's horror, it soon begins to turn terribly sour . . .

A fabulously spooky adventure set in the late-Victorian world of the music hall.

'Terrific characters' *TES*

'Fine's genius for storytelling reaches new heights: simple, direct, and with a subtle period feel to narrative and dialogue' *Independent*

Corgi Yearling
978 0 440 86630 5

www.**kidsatrandomhouse**.co.uk